D1314776

Sir Arthur Conan Doyle's

The Adventure of the Dancing Men

Adapted by: Vincent Goodwin

Illustrated by: Ben Dunn

magic
Wagon

visit us at
www.abdopublishing.com

Published by Magic Wagon, a division of the ABDO Group, 8000 West 78th Street, Edina, Minnesota, 55439.

Printed in the United States of America, North Mankato, Minnesota.
102009
012010

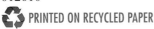

PRINTED ON RECYCLED PAPER

Original novel by Sir Arthur Conan Doyle
Adapted by Vincent Goodwin
Illustrated by Ben Dunn
Colored by Robby Bevard
Edited by Stephanie Hedlund and Rochelle Baltzer
Interior layout and design by Antarctic Press
Cover art by Ben Dunn
Cover design by Abbey Fitzgerald

Library of Congress Cataloging-in-Publication Data

Goodwin, Vincent.
Sir Arthur Conan Doyle's The adventure of the dancing men / adapted by Vincent Goodwin ; illustrated by Ben Dunn.
p. cm. -- (The graphic novel adventures of Sherlock Holmes)
Summary: Retells in graphic novel format a story featuring the great English detective Sherlock Holmes.
Includes bibliographical references.
ISBN 978-1-60270-723-8
1. Graphic novels. [1. Graphic novels. 2. Doyle, Arthur Conan, Sir, 1859-1930. Adventure of the Dancing Men—Adaptations. 3. Mystery and detective stories.] I. Dunn, Ben, ill. II. Doyle, Arthur Conan, Sir, 1859-1930. Adventure of the Dancing Men. III. Title. IV. Title: Adventure of the Dancing Men.

PZ7.7.G66Si 2010
741.5'973--dc22

2009032457

Table of Contents

Cast

Sherlock Holmes

Dr. John Watson

Hilton Cubitt

Mrs. Elsie Cubitt

Inspector Martin

Abe Slaney

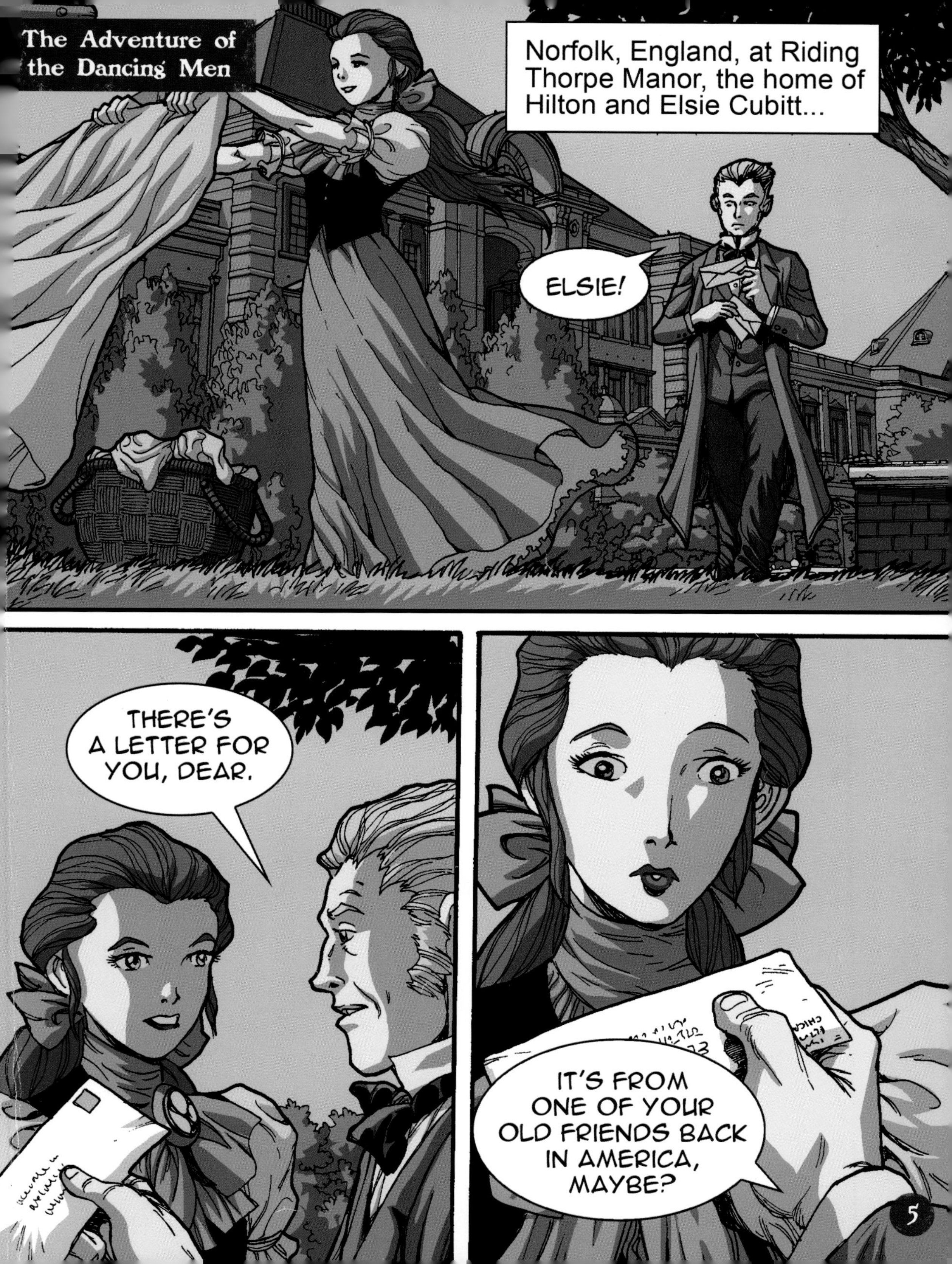

The Adventure of the Dancing Men
Norfolk, England, at Riding Thorpe Manor, the home of Hilton and Elsie Cubitt...
ELSIE!
THERE'S A LETTER FOR YOU, DEAR.
IT'S FROM ONE OF YOUR OLD FRIENDS BACK IN AMERICA, MAYBE?

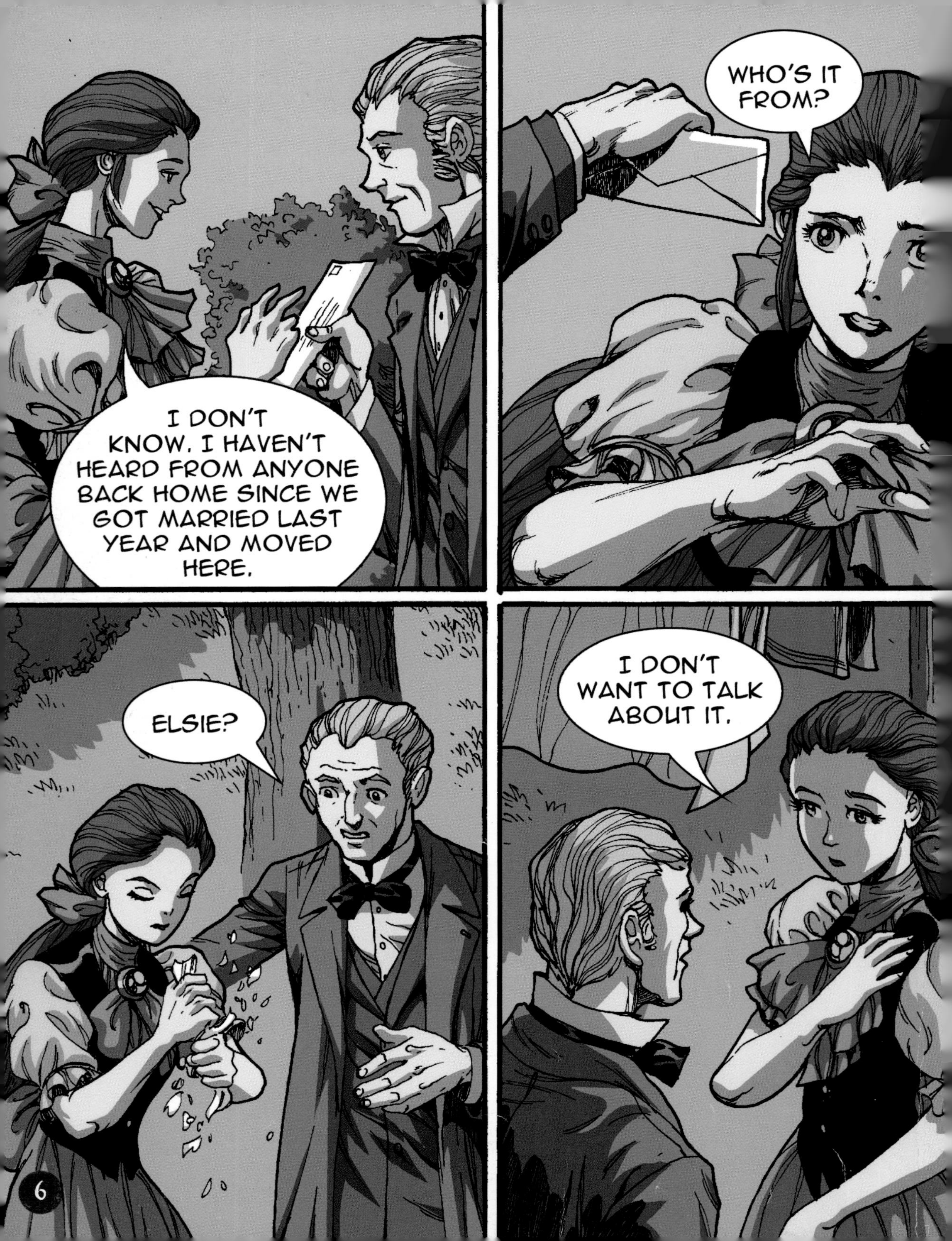
I DON'T KNOW. I HAVEN'T HEARD FROM ANYONE BACK HOME SINCE WE GOT MARRIED LAST YEAR AND MOVED HERE.
WHO'S IT FROM?
ELSIE?
I DON'T WANT TO TALK ABOUT IT.

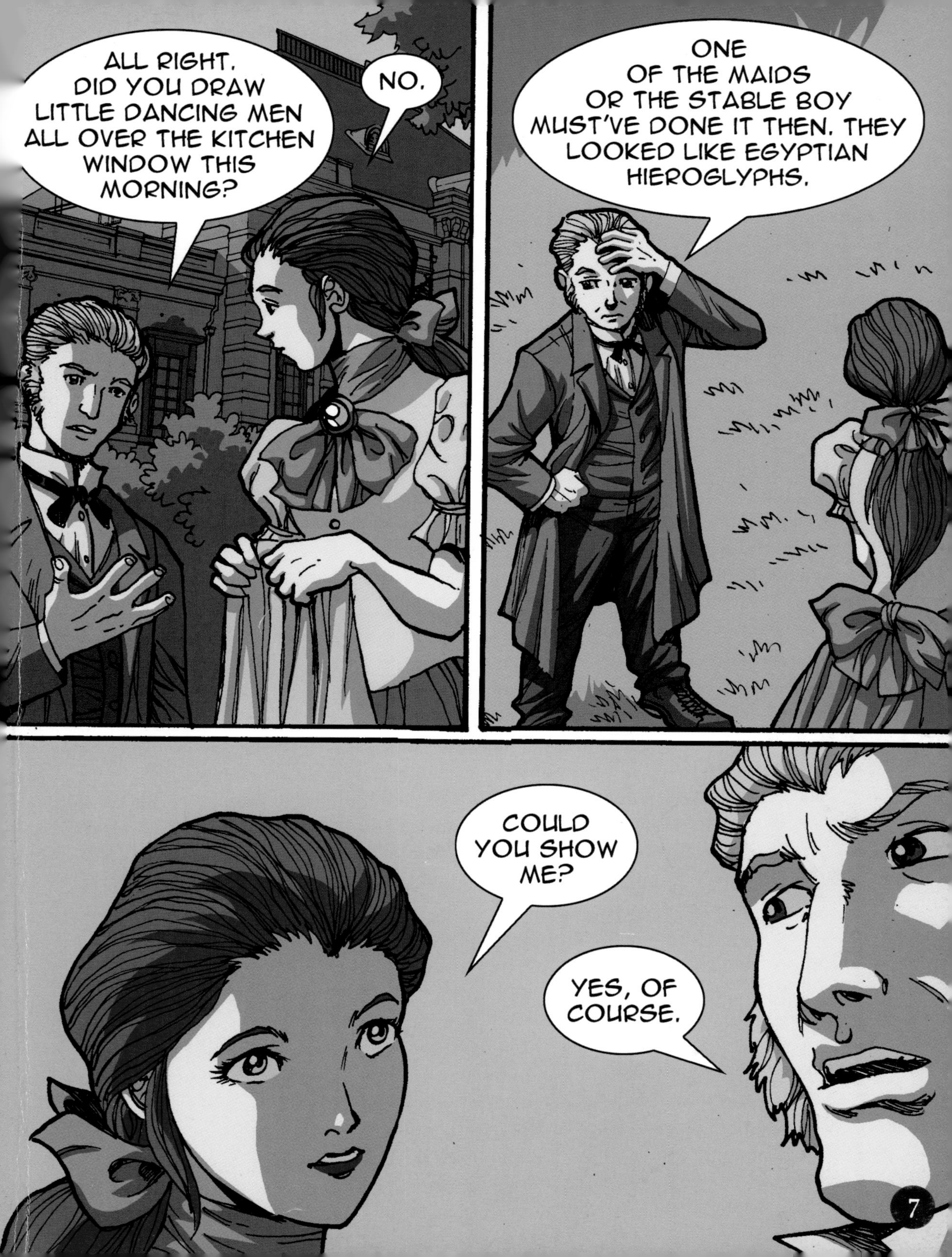
ALL RIGHT. DID YOU DRAW LITTLE DANCING MEN ALL OVER THE KITCHEN WINDOW THIS MORNING?
NO.
ONE OF THE MAIDS OR THE STABLE BOY MUST'VE DONE IT THEN. THEY LOOKED LIKE EGYPTIAN HIEROGLYPHS.
COULD YOU SHOW ME?
YES, OF COURSE.

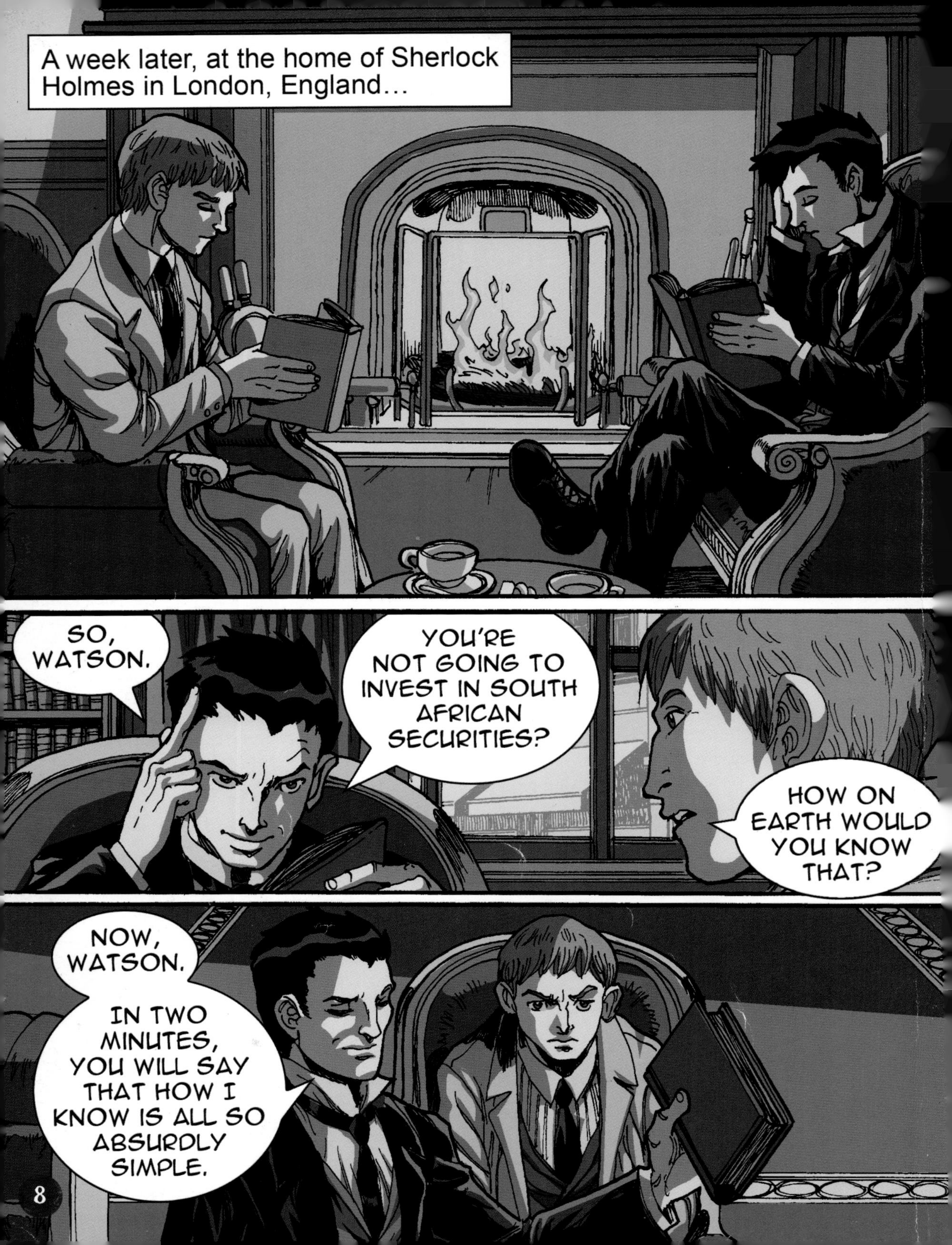
A week later, at the home of Sherlock Holmes in London, England…
SO, WATSON.
YOU'RE NOT GOING TO INVEST IN SOUTH AFRICAN SECURITIES?
HOW ON EARTH WOULD YOU KNOW THAT?
NOW, WATSON.
IN TWO MINUTES, YOU WILL SAY THAT HOW I KNOW IS ALL SO ABSURDLY SIMPLE.

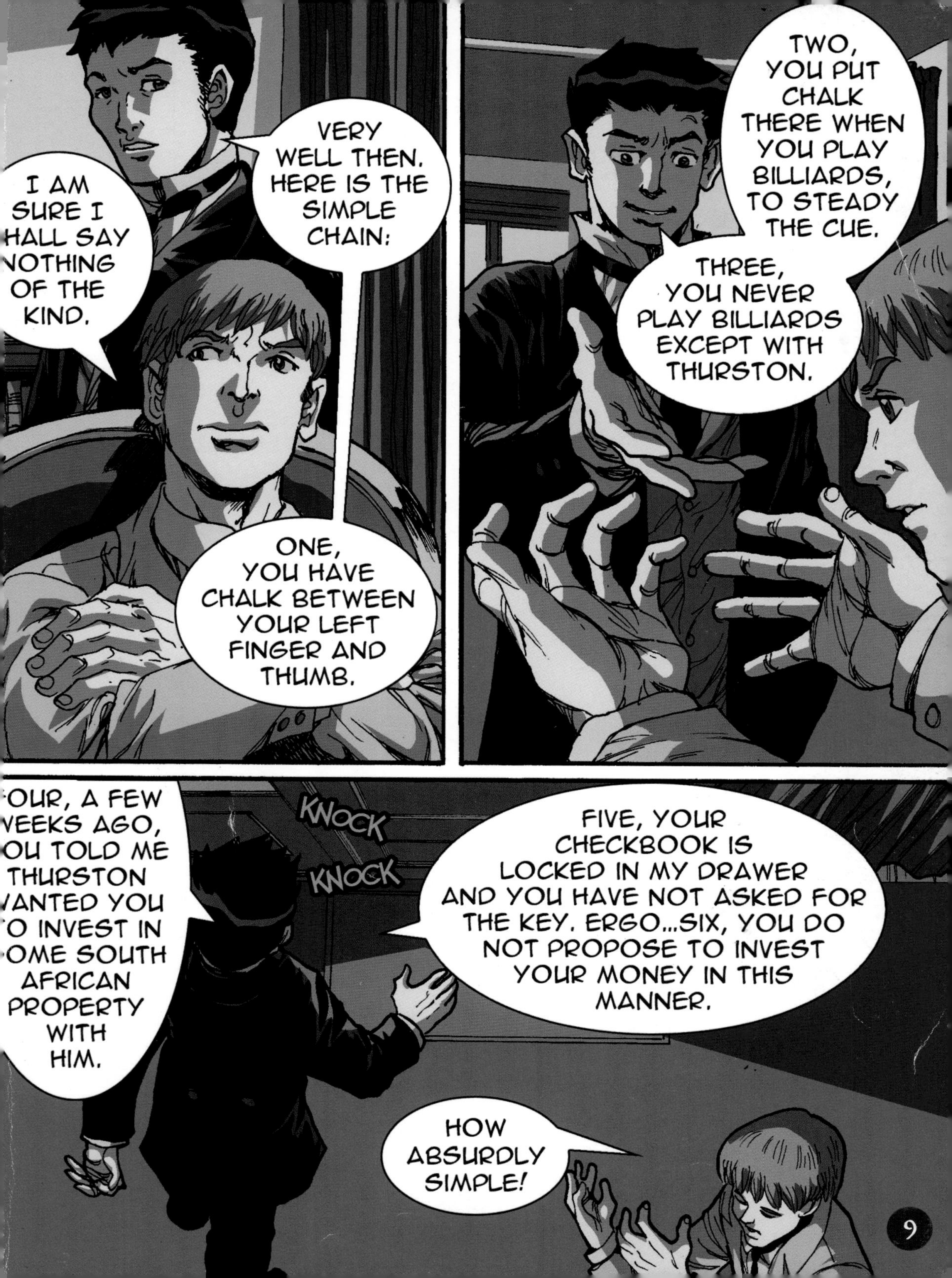
I AM SURE I HALL SAY NOTHING OF THE KIND.
VERY WELL THEN. HERE IS THE SIMPLE CHAIN:
ONE, YOU HAVE CHALK BETWEEN YOUR LEFT FINGER AND THUMB.
TWO, YOU PUT CHALK THERE WHEN YOU PLAY BILLIARDS, TO STEADY THE CUE.
THREE, YOU NEVER PLAY BILLIARDS EXCEPT WITH THURSTON.
OUR, A FEW EEKS AGO, OU TOLD ME THURSTON ANTED YOU O INVEST IN OME SOUTH AFRICAN PROPERTY WITH HIM.
KNOCK
KNOCK
FIVE, YOUR CHECKBOOK IS LOCKED IN MY DRAWER AND YOU HAVE NOT ASKED FOR THE KEY. ERGO...SIX, YOU DO NOT PROPOSE TO INVEST YOUR MONEY IN THIS MANNER.
HOW ABSURDLY SIMPLE!

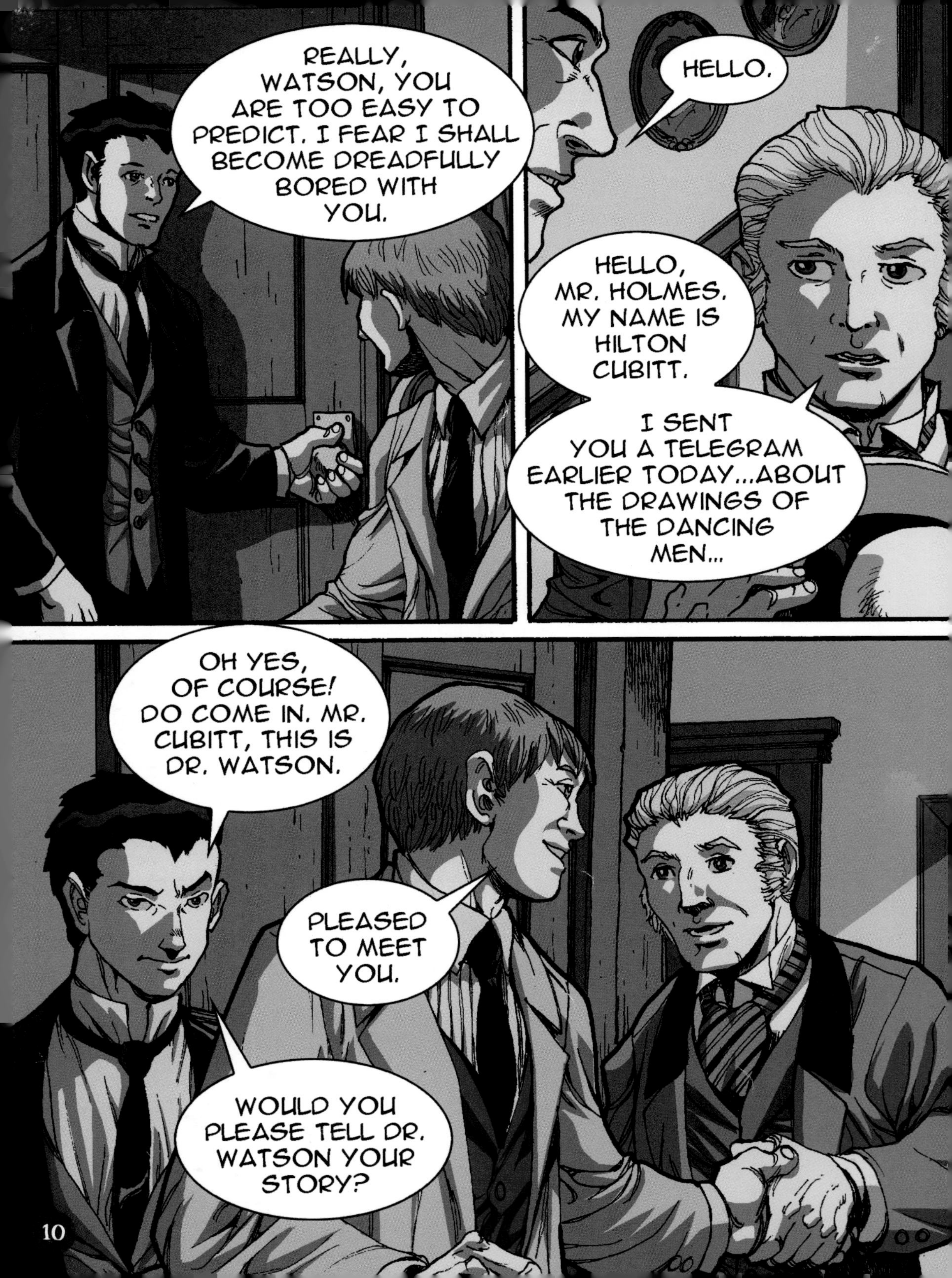
REALLY, WATSON, YOU ARE TOO EASY TO PREDICT. I FEAR I SHALL BECOME DREADFULLY BORED WITH YOU.
HELLO.
HELLO, MR. HOLMES. MY NAME IS HILTON CUBITT.
I SENT YOU A TELEGRAM EARLIER TODAY...ABOUT THE DRAWINGS OF THE DANCING MEN...
OH YES, OF COURSE! DO COME IN. MR. CUBITT, THIS IS DR. WATSON.
PLEASED TO MEET YOU.
WOULD YOU PLEASE TELL DR. WATSON YOUR STORY?

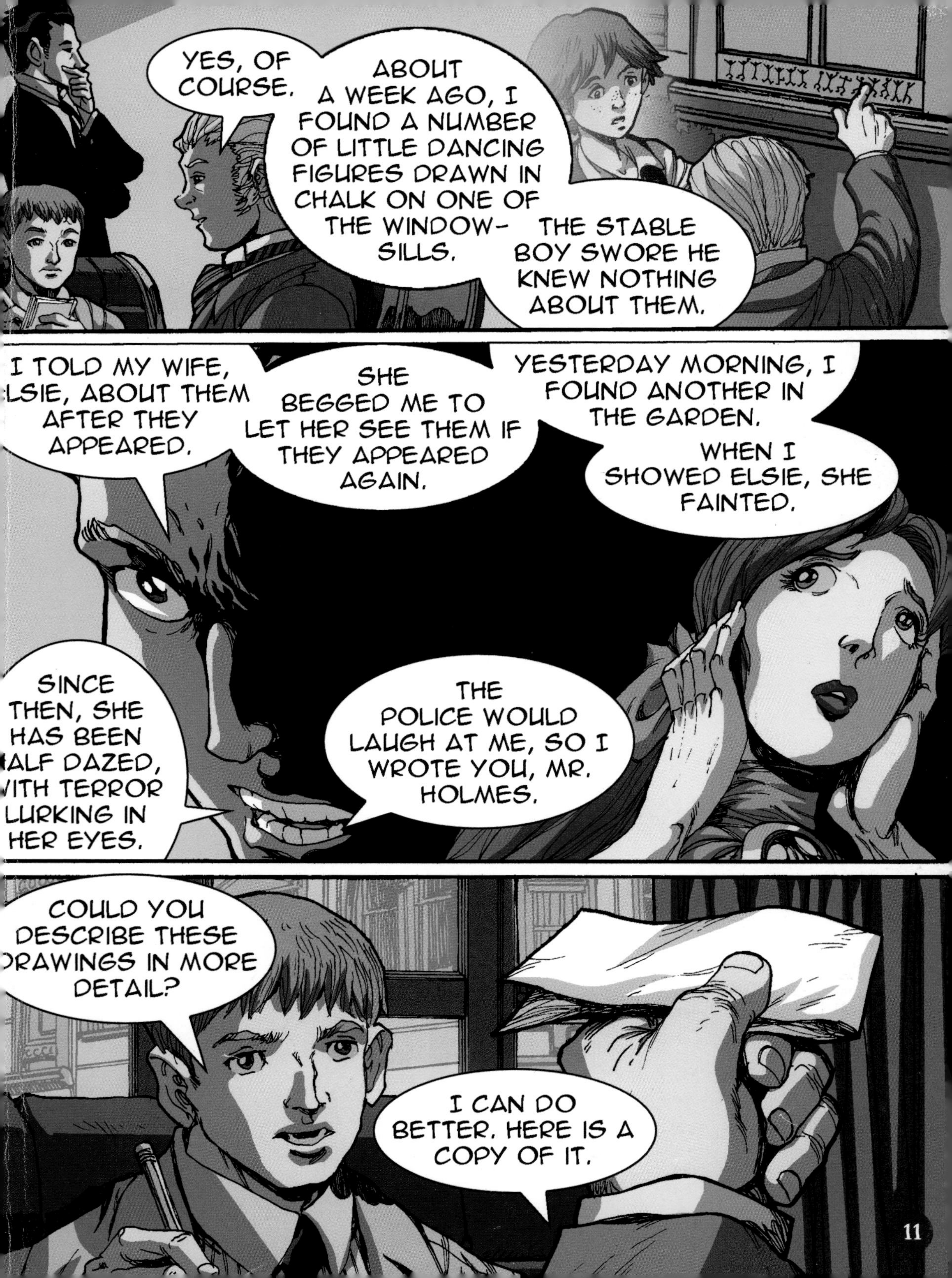
YES, OF COURSE.
ABOUT A WEEK AGO, I FOUND A NUMBER OF LITTLE DANCING FIGURES DRAWN IN CHALK ON ONE OF THE WINDOW-SILLS.
THE STABLE BOY SWORE HE KNEW NOTHING ABOUT THEM.
I TOLD MY WIFE, LSIE, ABOUT THEM AFTER THEY APPEARED.
SHE BEGGED ME TO LET HER SEE THEM IF THEY APPEARED AGAIN.
YESTERDAY MORNING, I FOUND ANOTHER IN THE GARDEN.
WHEN I SHOWED ELSIE, SHE FAINTED.
SINCE THEN, SHE HAS BEEN ALF DAZED, ITH TERROR LURKING IN HER EYES.
THE POLICE WOULD LAUGH AT ME, SO I WROTE YOU, MR. HOLMES.
COULD YOU DESCRIBE THESE RAWINGS IN MORE DETAIL?
I CAN DO BETTER. HERE IS A COPY OF IT.

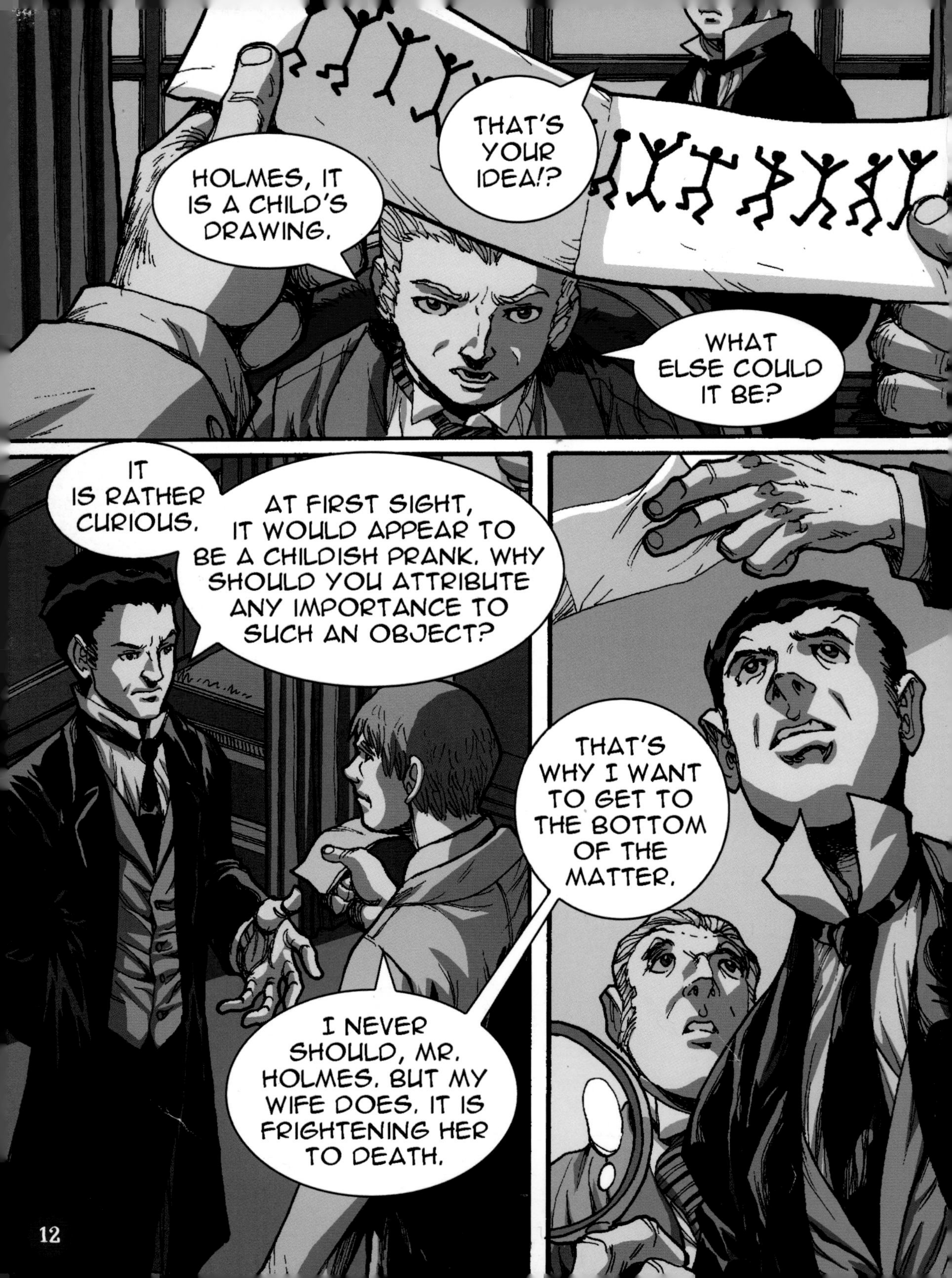
HOLMES, IT IS A CHILD'S DRAWING.
THAT'S YOUR IDEA!?
WHAT ELSE COULD IT BE?
IT IS RATHER CURIOUS.
AT FIRST SIGHT, IT WOULD APPEAR TO BE A CHILDISH PRANK. WHY SHOULD YOU ATTRIBUTE ANY IMPORTANCE TO SUCH AN OBJECT?
I NEVER SHOULD, MR. HOLMES. BUT MY WIFE DOES. IT IS FRIGHTENING HER TO DEATH.
THAT'S WHY I WANT TO GET TO THE BOTTOM OF THE MATTER.

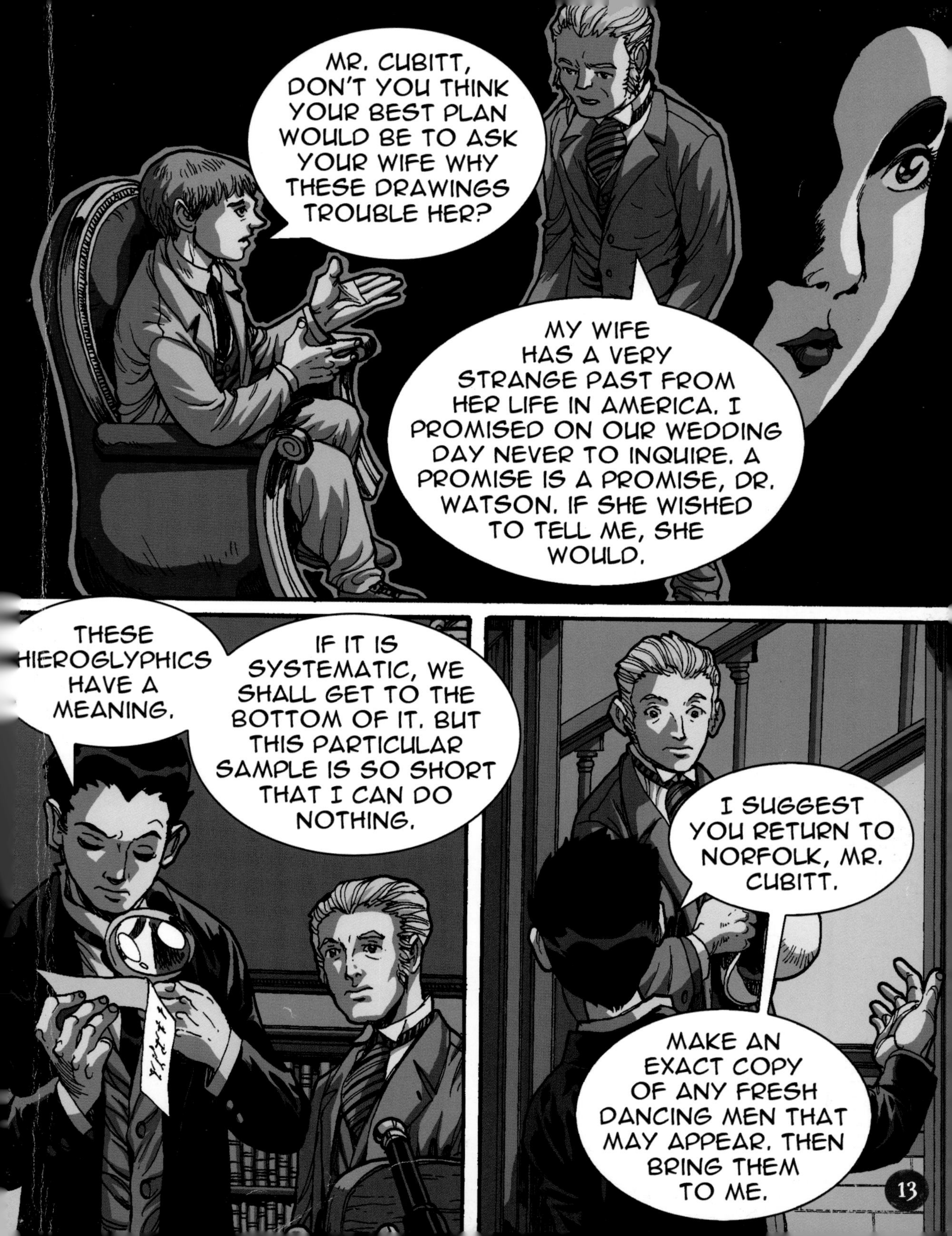
MR. CUBITT, DON'T YOU THINK YOUR BEST PLAN WOULD BE TO ASK YOUR WIFE WHY THESE DRAWINGS TROUBLE HER?
MY WIFE HAS A VERY STRANGE PAST FROM HER LIFE IN AMERICA. I PROMISED ON OUR WEDDING DAY NEVER TO INQUIRE. A PROMISE IS A PROMISE, DR. WATSON. IF SHE WISHED TO TELL ME, SHE WOULD.
THESE HIEROGLYPHICS HAVE A MEANING.
IF IT IS SYSTEMATIC, WE SHALL GET TO THE BOTTOM OF IT. BUT THIS PARTICULAR SAMPLE IS SO SHORT THAT I CAN DO NOTHING.
I SUGGEST YOU RETURN TO NORFOLK, MR. CUBITT.
MAKE AN EXACT COPY OF ANY FRESH DANCING MEN THAT MAY APPEAR. THEN BRING THEM TO ME.

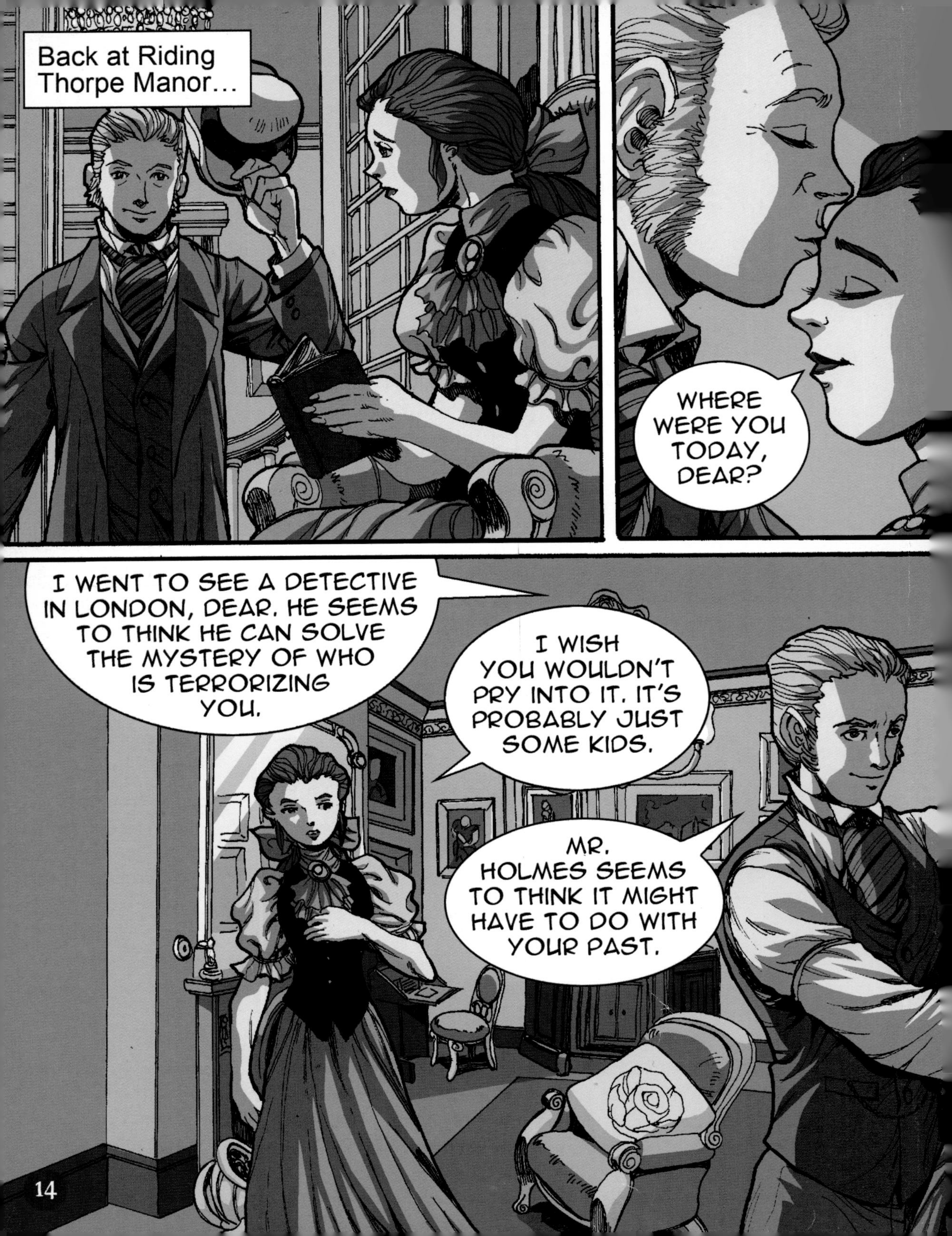
Back at Riding Thorpe Manor…
WHERE WERE YOU TODAY, DEAR?
I WENT TO SEE A DETECTIVE IN LONDON, DEAR. HE SEEMS TO THINK HE CAN SOLVE THE MYSTERY OF WHO IS TERRORIZING YOU.
I WISH YOU WOULDN'T PRY INTO IT. IT'S PROBABLY JUST SOME KIDS.
MR. HOLMES SEEMS TO THINK IT MIGHT HAVE TO DO WITH YOUR PAST.

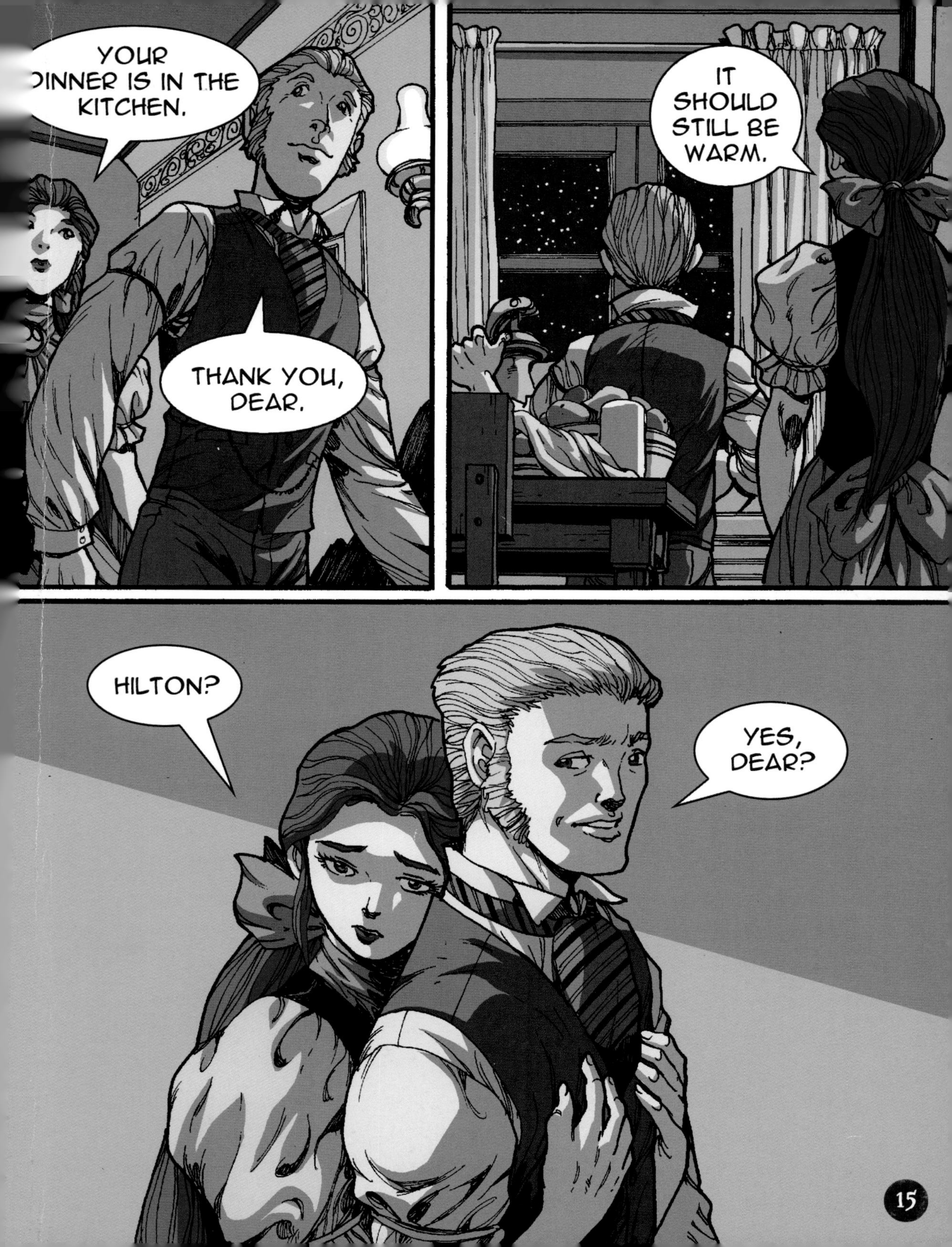
YOUR DINNER IS IN THE KITCHEN.
THANK YOU, DEAR.
IT SHOULD STILL BE WARM.
HILTON?
YES, DEAR?

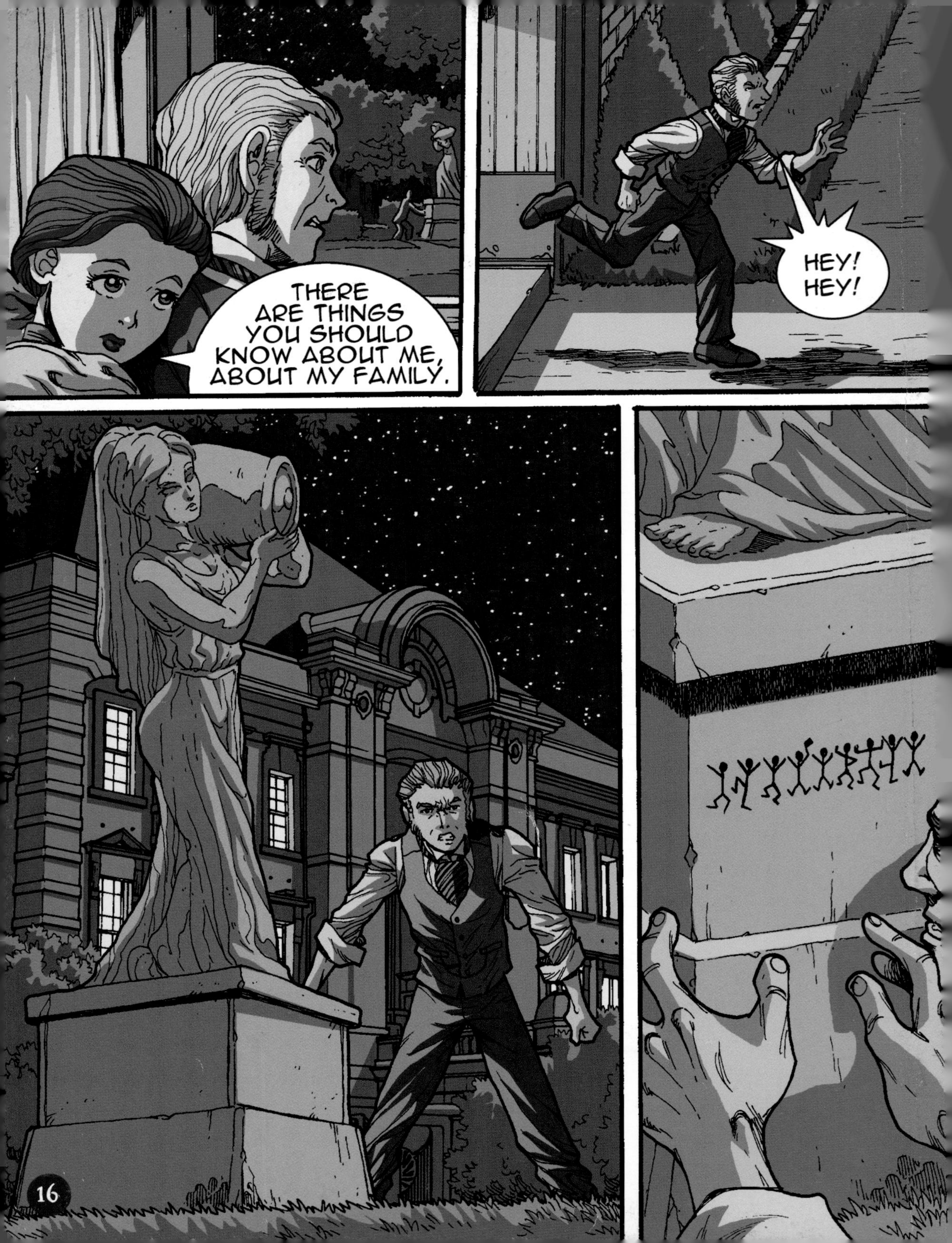
THERE ARE THINGS YOU SHOULD KNOW ABOUT ME, ABOUT MY FAMILY.
HEY! HEY!

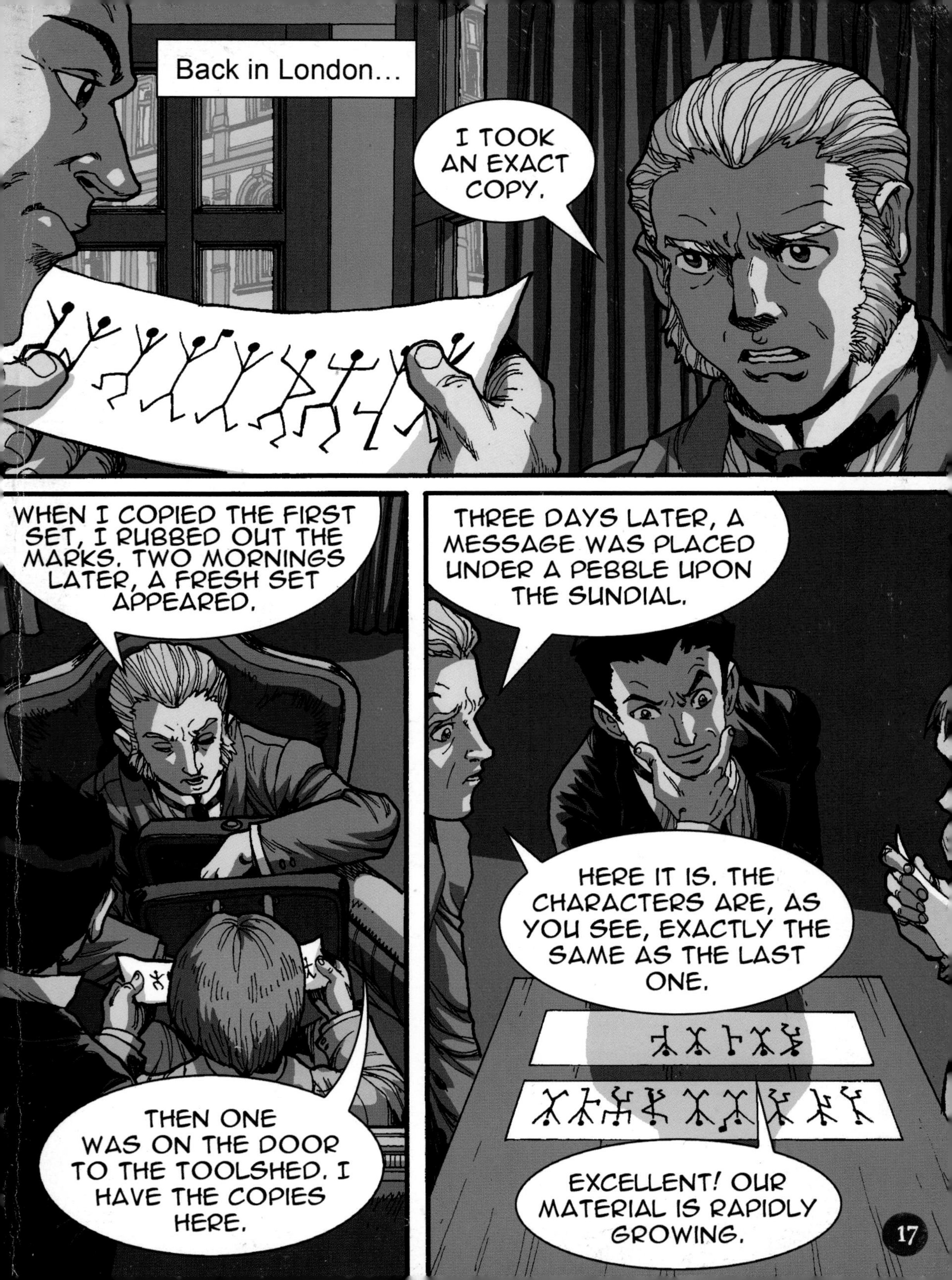
Back in London…
I TOOK AN EXACT COPY.
WHEN I COPIED THE FIRST SET, I RUBBED OUT THE MARKS. TWO MORNINGS LATER, A FRESH SET APPEARED.
THEN ONE WAS ON THE DOOR TO THE TOOLSHED. I HAVE THE COPIES HERE.
THREE DAYS LATER, A MESSAGE WAS PLACED UNDER A PEBBLE UPON THE SUNDIAL.
HERE IT IS. THE CHARACTERS ARE, AS YOU SEE, EXACTLY THE SAME AS THE LAST ONE.
EXCELLENT! OUR MATERIAL IS RAPIDLY GROWING.

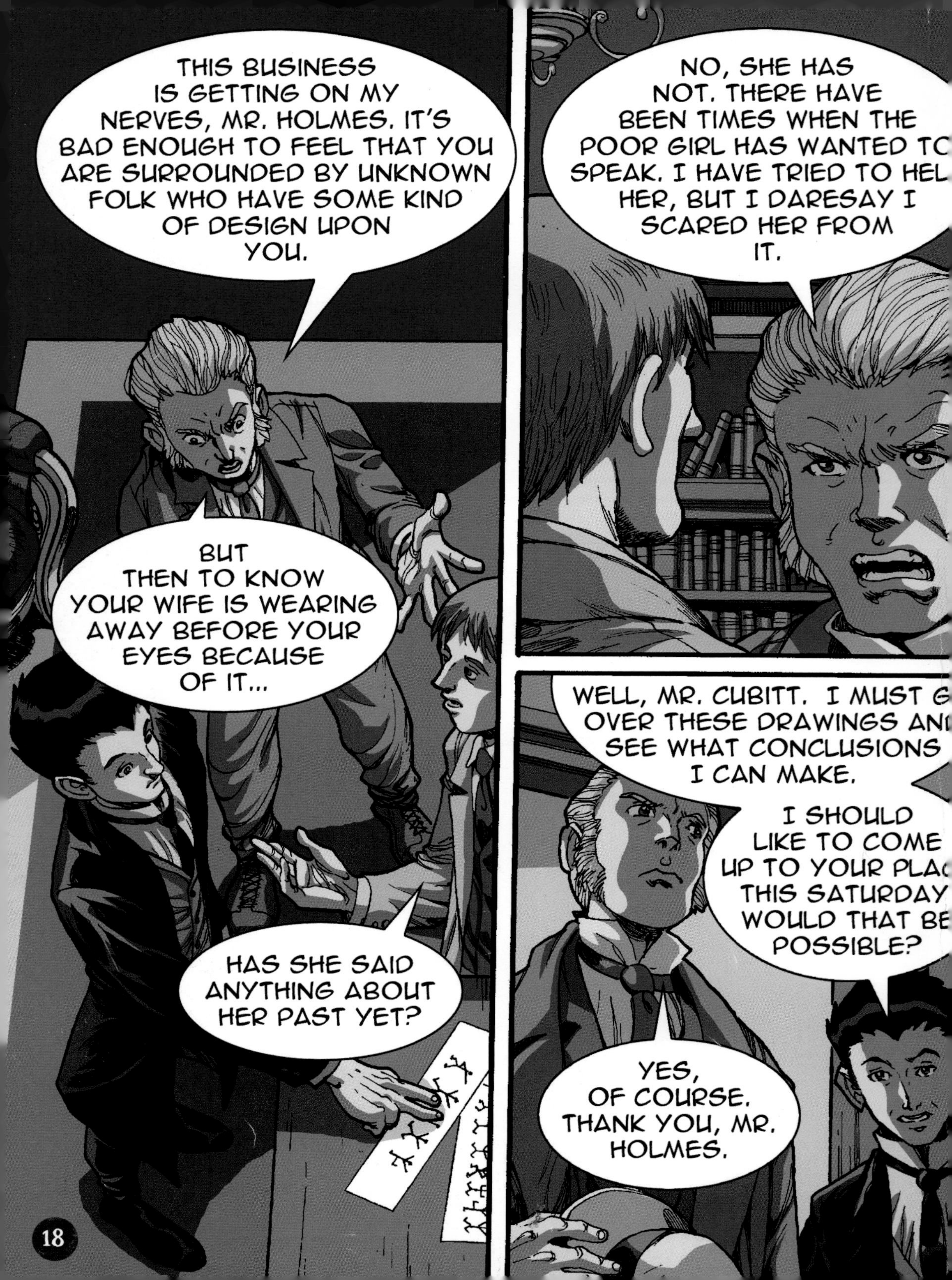
THIS BUSINESS IS GETTING ON MY NERVES, MR. HOLMES. IT'S BAD ENOUGH TO FEEL THAT YOU ARE SURROUNDED BY UNKNOWN FOLK WHO HAVE SOME KIND OF DESIGN UPON YOU.
BUT THEN TO KNOW YOUR WIFE IS WEARING AWAY BEFORE YOUR EYES BECAUSE OF IT...
HAS SHE SAID ANYTHING ABOUT HER PAST YET?
NO, SHE HAS NOT. THERE HAVE BEEN TIMES WHEN THE POOR GIRL HAS WANTED TO SPEAK. I HAVE TRIED TO HEL HER, BUT I DARESAY I SCARED HER FROM IT.
WELL, MR. CUBITT. I MUST G OVER THESE DRAWINGS AN SEE WHAT CONCLUSIONS I CAN MAKE.
I SHOULD LIKE TO COME UP TO YOUR PLA THIS SATURDAY WOULD THAT BE POSSIBLE?
YES, OF COURSE. THANK YOU, MR. HOLMES.

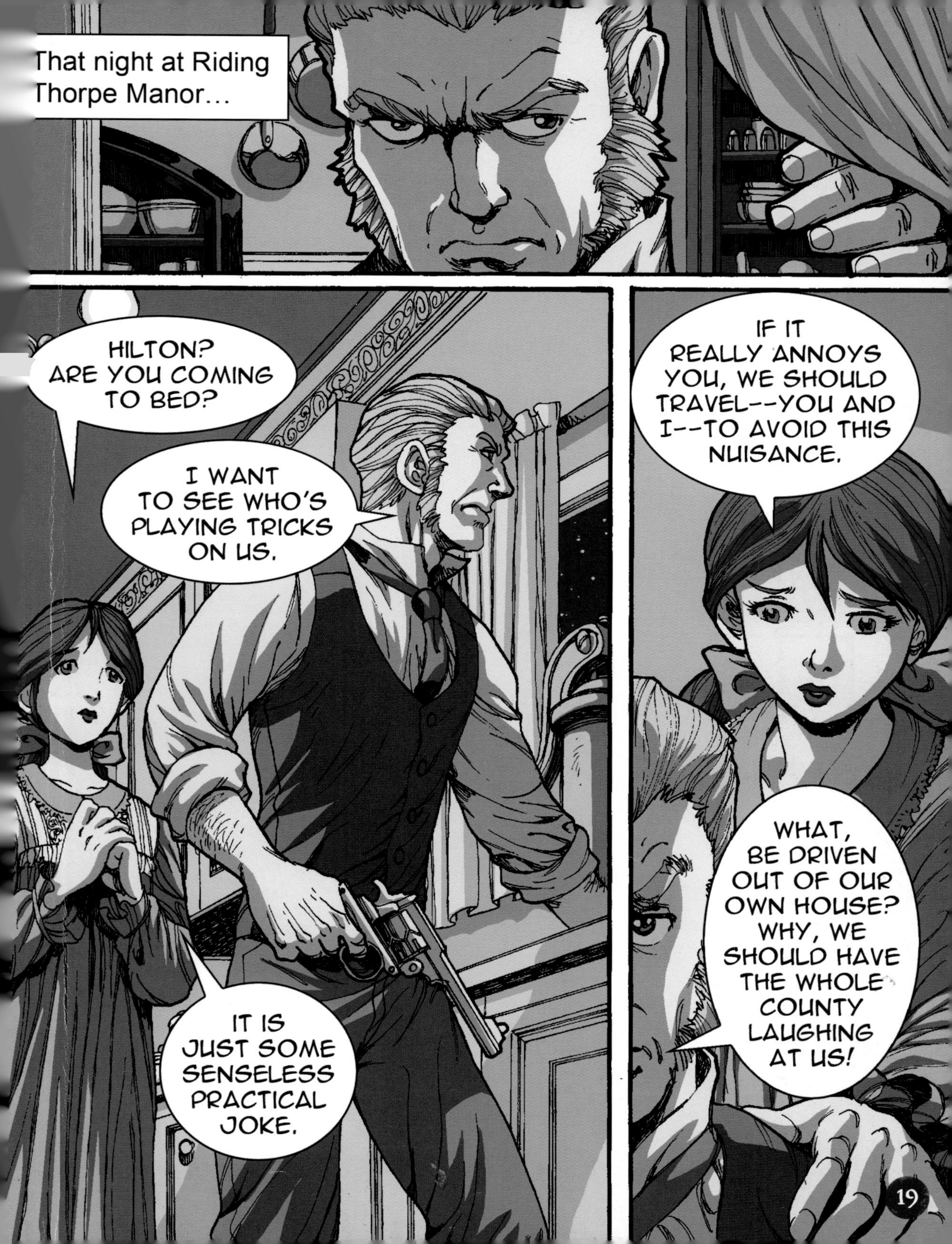
That night at Riding Thorpe Manor…
HILTON? ARE YOU COMING TO BED?
I WANT TO SEE WHO'S PLAYING TRICKS ON US.
IT IS JUST SOME SENSELESS PRACTICAL JOKE.
IF IT REALLY ANNOYS YOU, WE SHOULD TRAVEL--YOU AND I--TO AVOID THIS NUISANCE.
WHAT, BE DRIVEN OUT OF OUR OWN HOUSE? WHY, WE SHOULD HAVE THE WHOLE COUNTY LAUGHING AT US!

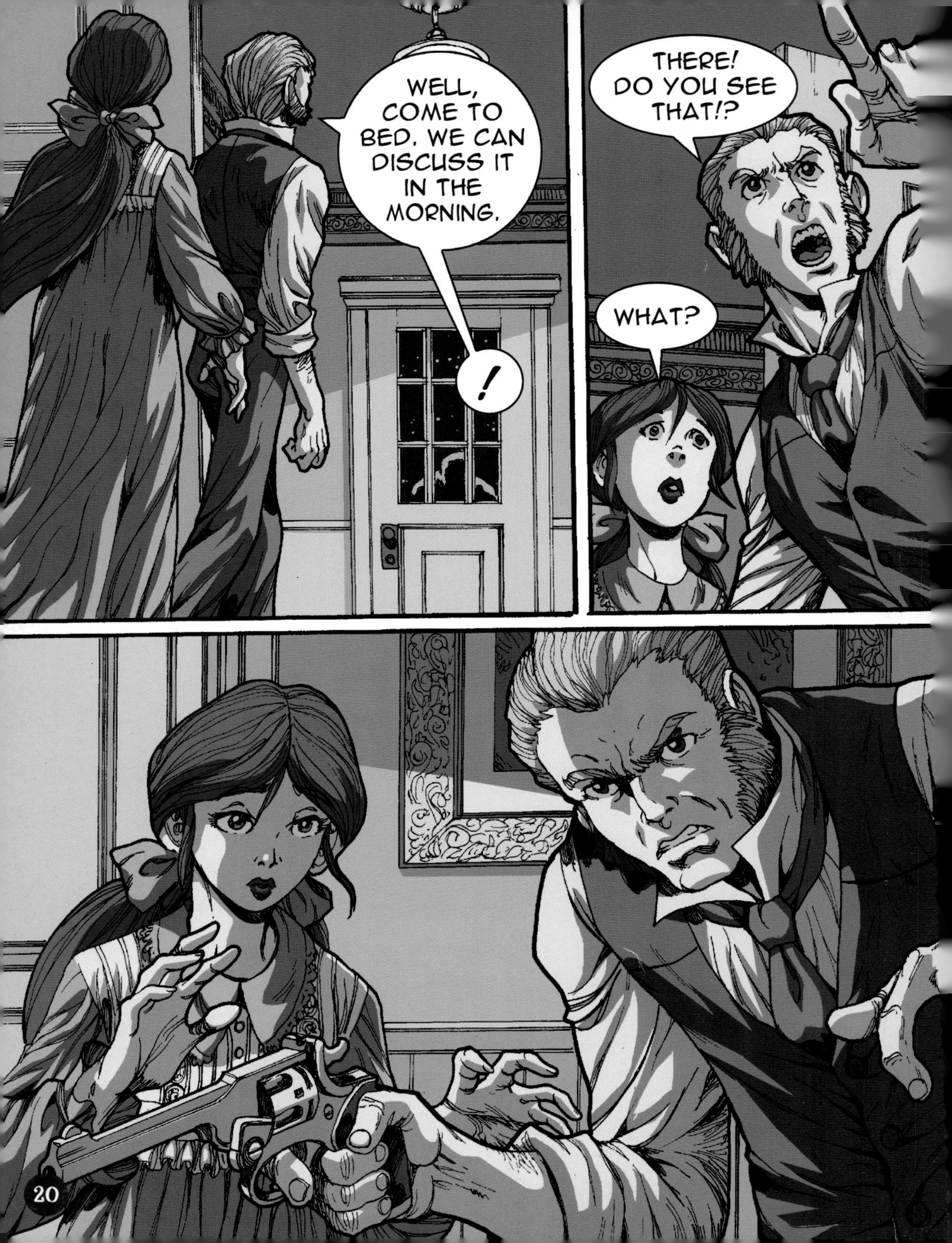
WELL, COME TO BED. WE CAN DISCUSS IT IN THE MORNING.
!
THERE! DO YOU SEE THAT!?
WHAT?

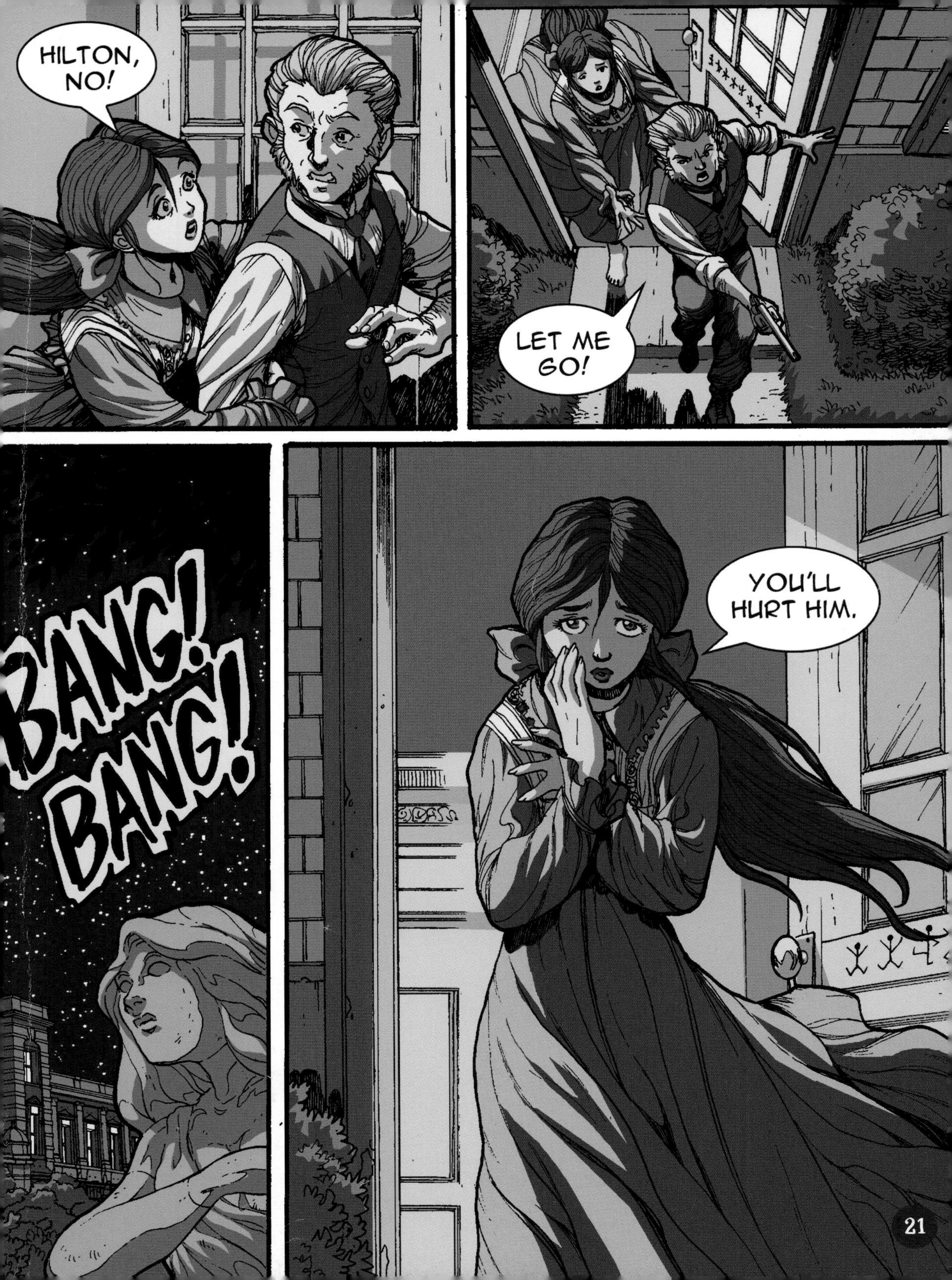
HILTON, NO!
LET ME GO!
BANG! BANG!
YOU'LL HURT HIM.

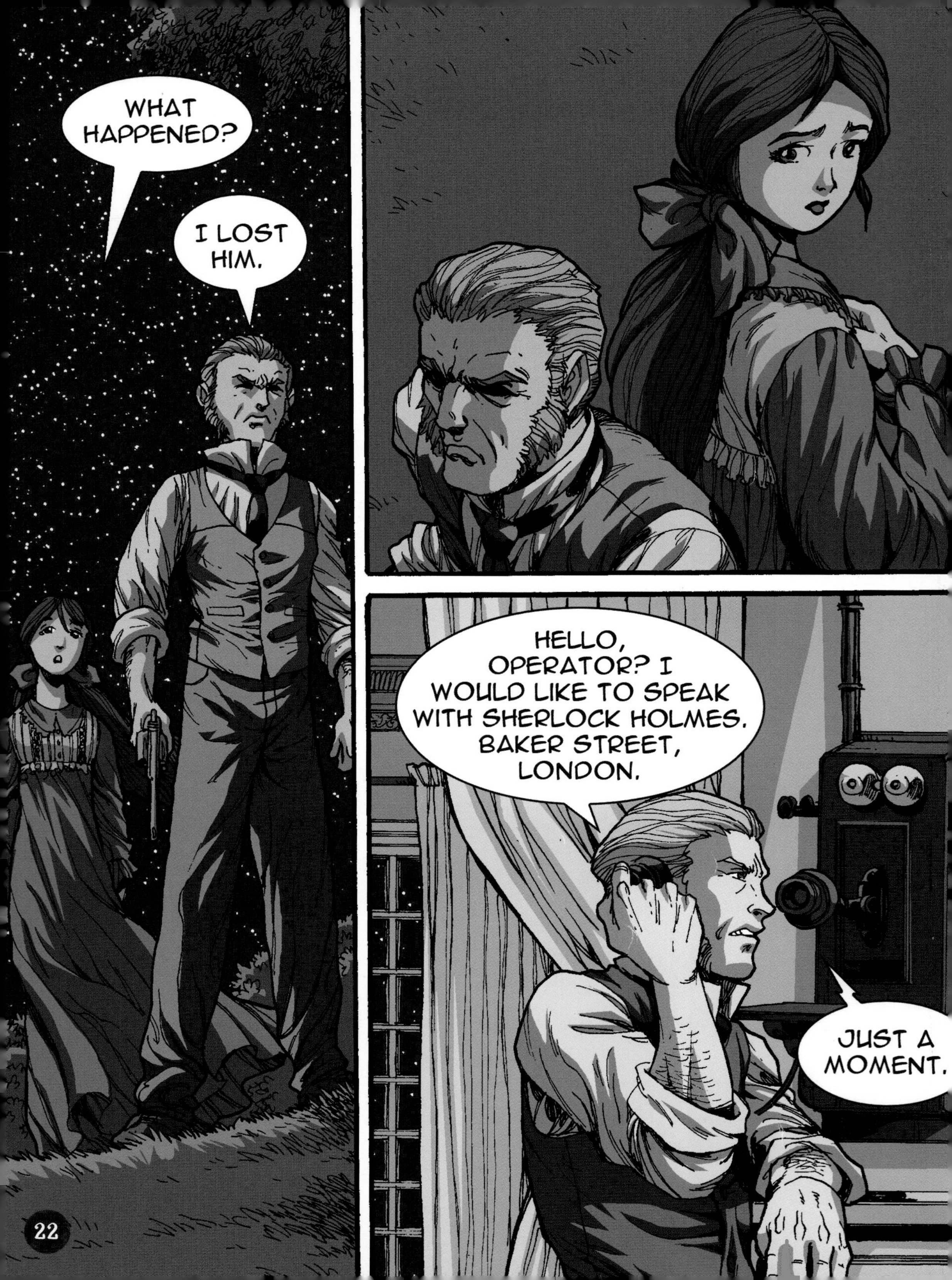
WHAT HAPPENED?
I LOST HIM.
HELLO, OPERATOR? I WOULD LIKE TO SPEAK WITH SHERLOCK HOLMES. BAKER STREET, LONDON.
JUST A MOMENT.

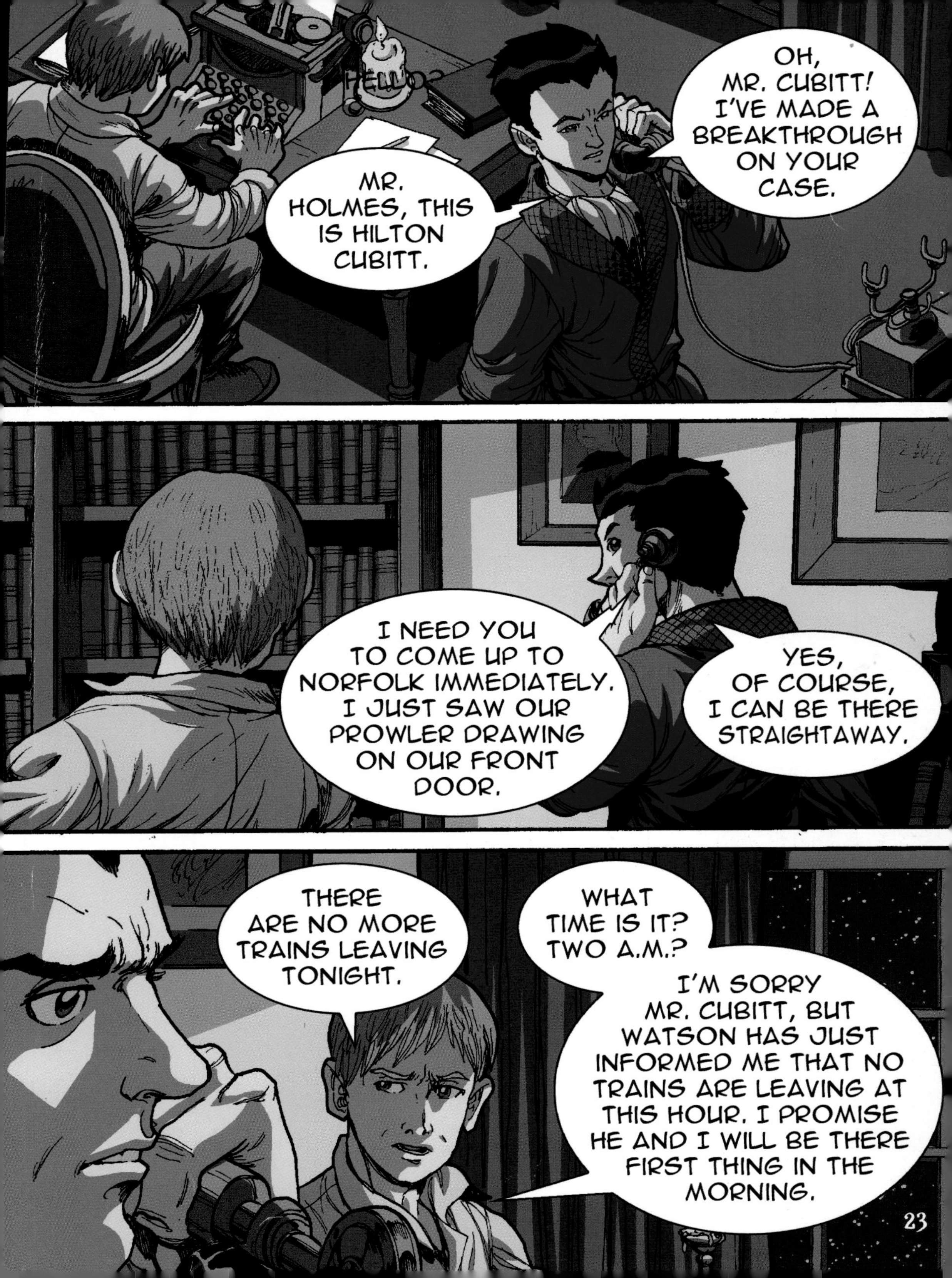
HELLO?
MR. HOLMES, THIS IS HILTON CUBITT.
OH, MR. CUBITT! I'VE MADE A BREAKTHROUGH ON YOUR CASE.
I NEED YOU TO COME UP TO NORFOLK IMMEDIATELY. I JUST SAW OUR PROWLER DRAWING ON OUR FRONT DOOR.
YES, OF COURSE, I CAN BE THERE STRAIGHTAWAY.
THERE ARE NO MORE TRAINS LEAVING TONIGHT.
WHAT TIME IS IT? TWO A.M.?
I'M SORRY MR. CUBITT, BUT WATSON HAS JUST INFORMED ME THAT NO TRAINS ARE LEAVING AT THIS HOUR. I PROMISE HE AND I WILL BE THERE FIRST THING IN THE MORNING.

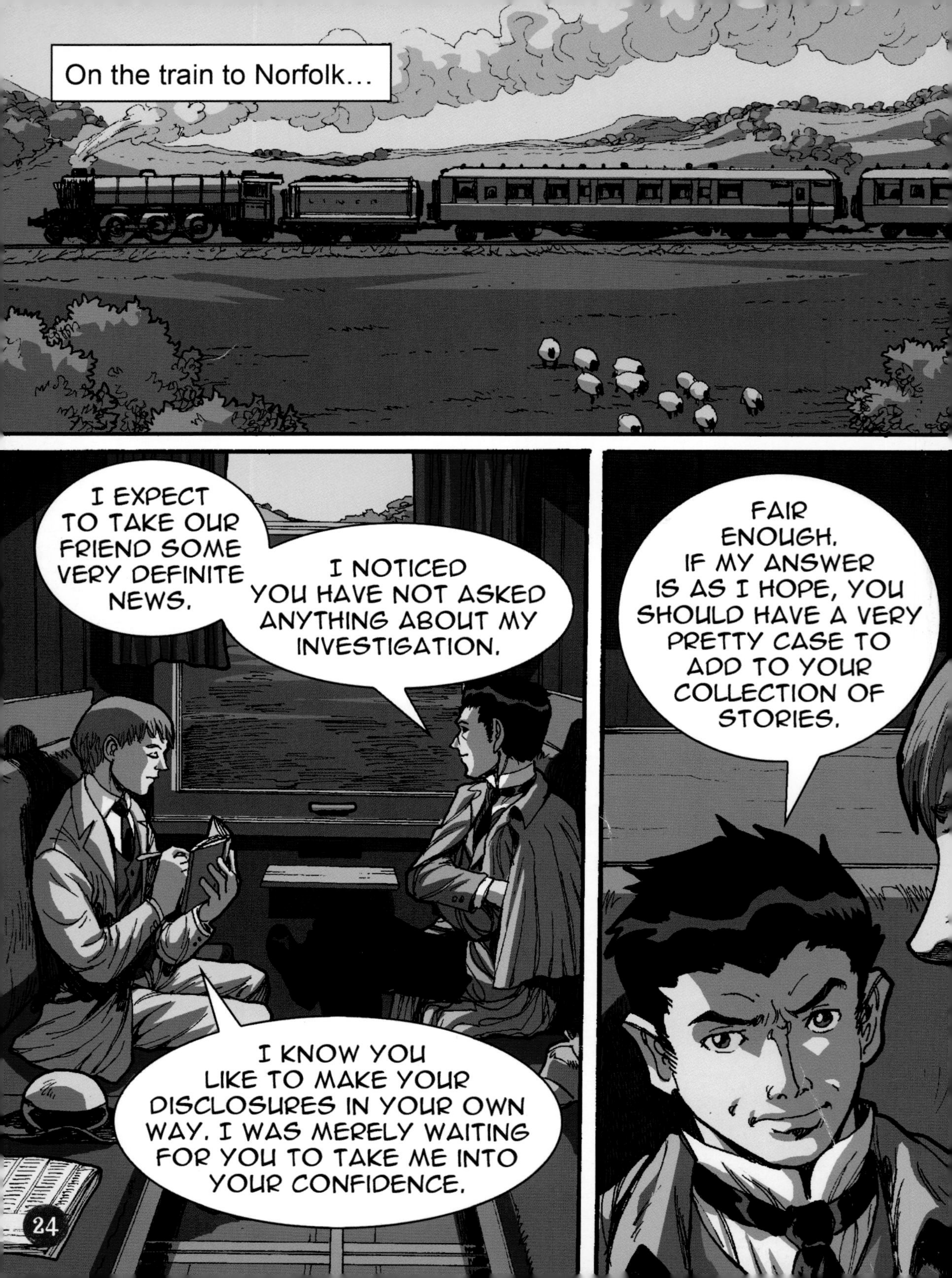
On the train to Norfolk…
I EXPECT TO TAKE OUR FRIEND SOME VERY DEFINITE NEWS.
I NOTICED YOU HAVE NOT ASKED ANYTHING ABOUT MY INVESTIGATION.
I KNOW YOU LIKE TO MAKE YOUR DISCLOSURES IN YOUR OWN WAY. I WAS MERELY WAITING FOR YOU TO TAKE ME INTO YOUR CONFIDENCE.
FAIR ENOUGH. IF MY ANSWER IS AS I HOPE, YOU SHOULD HAVE A VERY PRETTY CASE TO ADD TO YOUR COLLECTION OF STORIES.

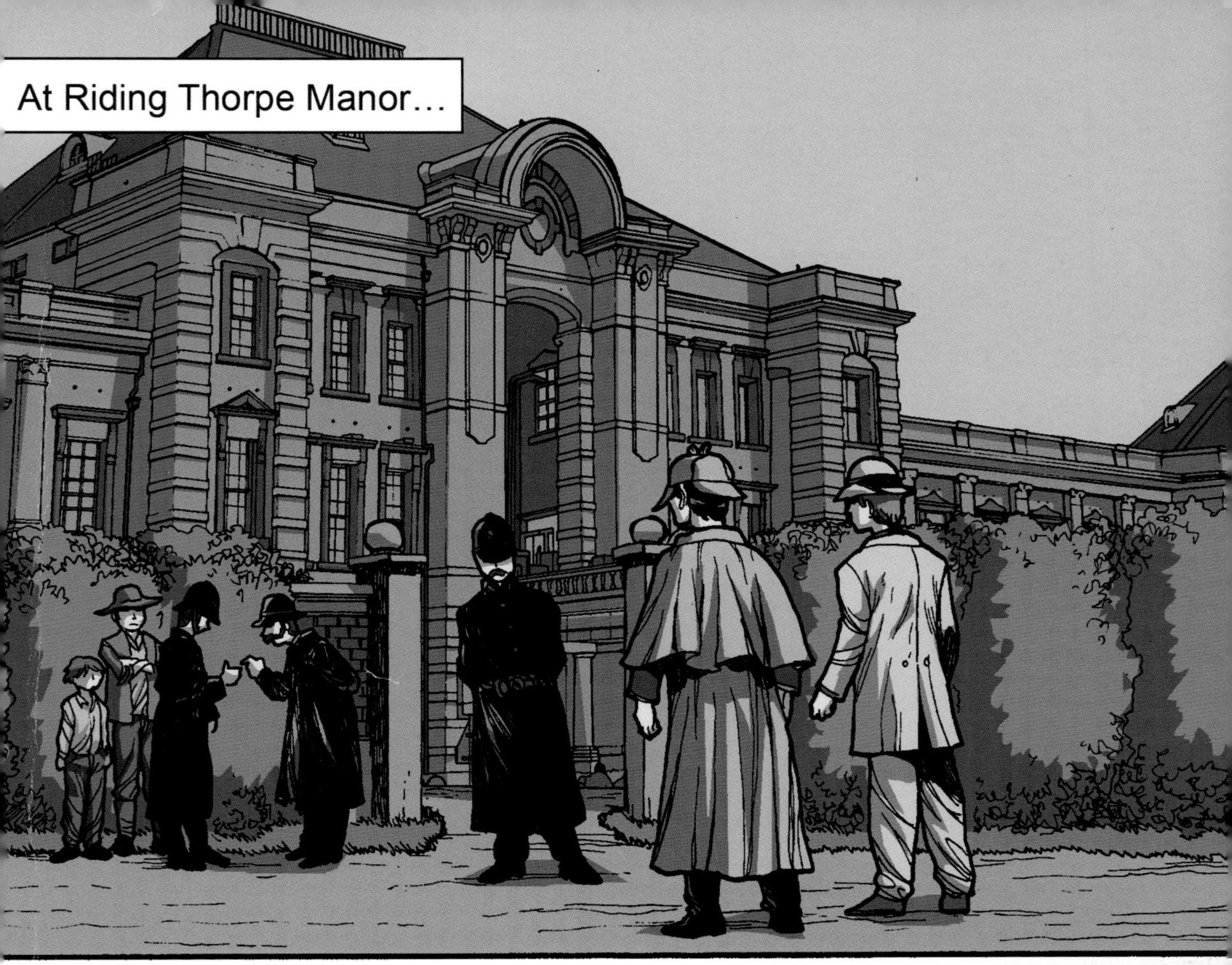
At Riding Thorpe Manor...

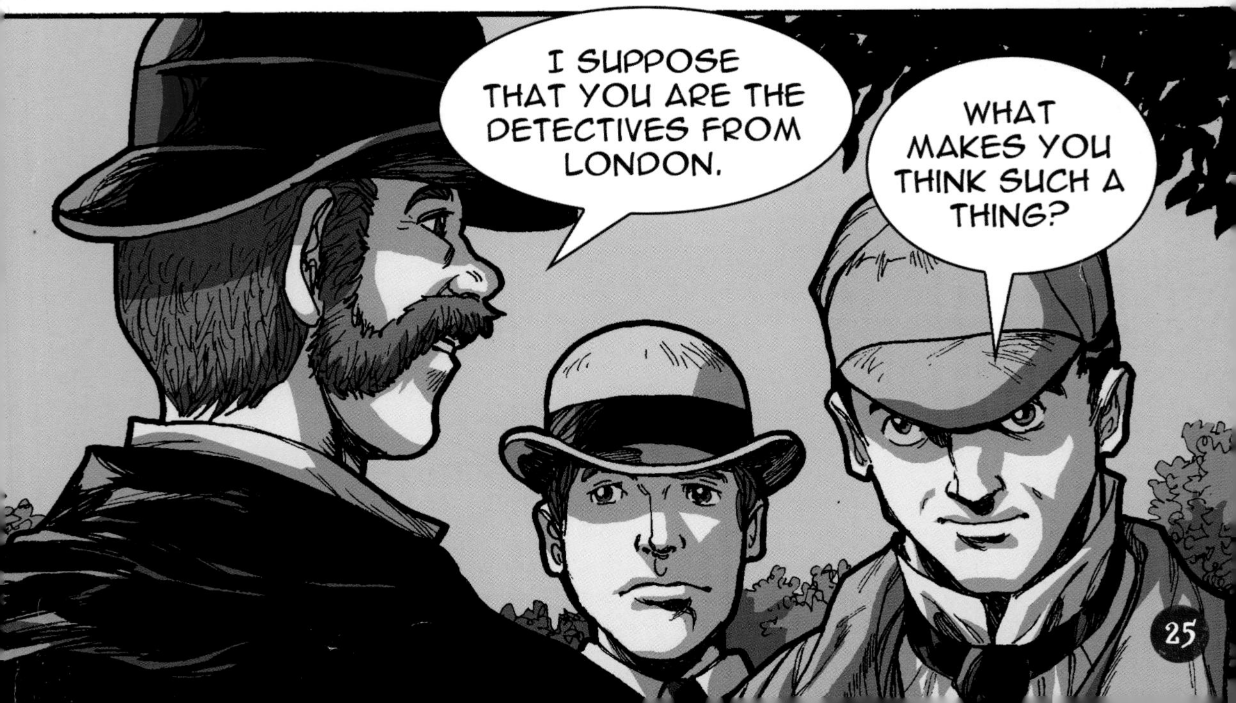
I SUPPOSE THAT YOU ARE THE DETECTIVES FROM LONDON.
WHAT MAKES YOU THINK SUCH A THING?

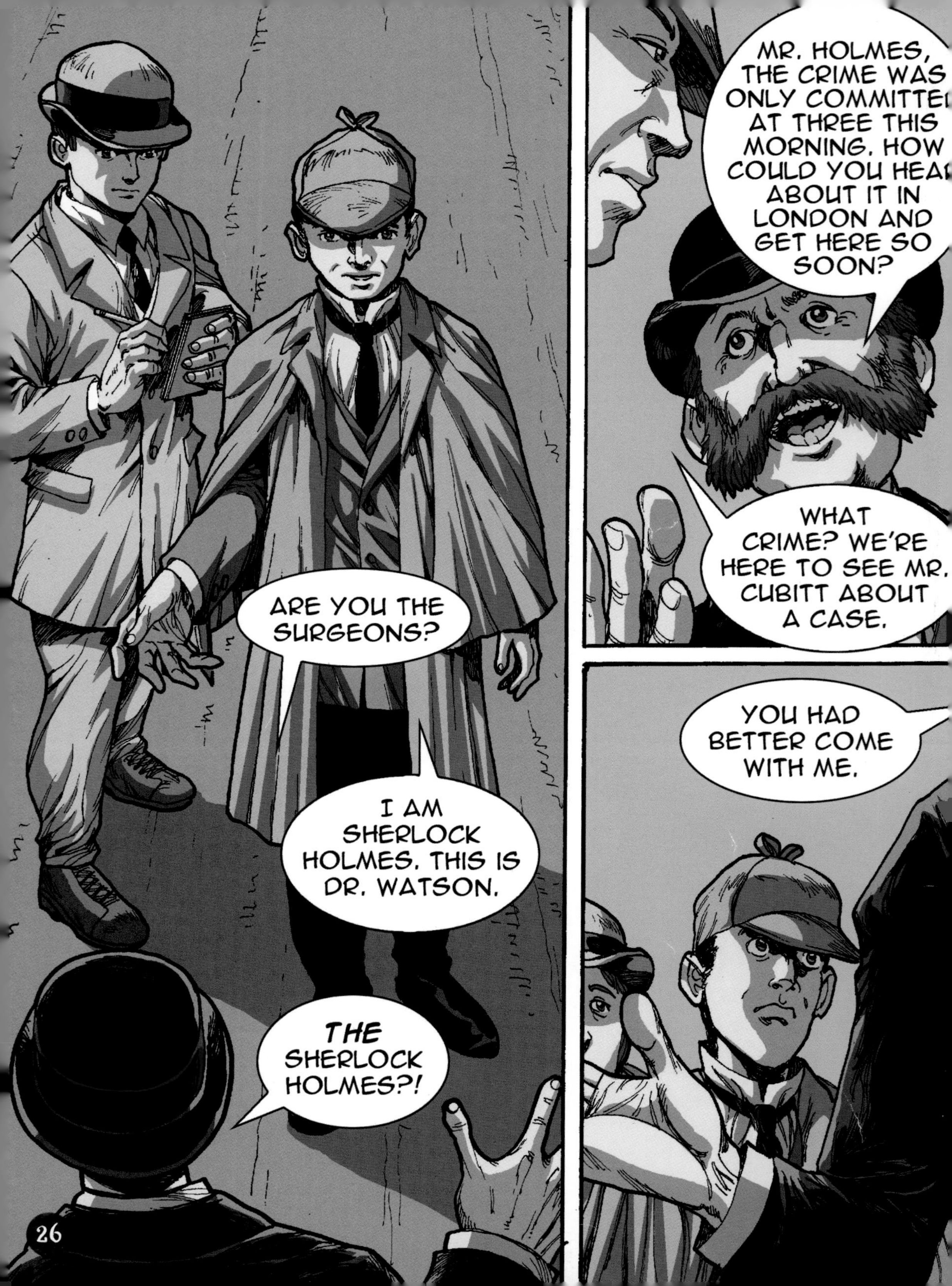
ARE YOU THE SURGEONS?
I AM SHERLOCK HOLMES. THIS IS DR. WATSON.
THE SHERLOCK HOLMES?!
MR. HOLMES, THE CRIME WAS ONLY COMMITTE AT THREE THIS MORNING. HOW COULD YOU HEA ABOUT IT IN LONDON AND GET HERE SO SOON?
WHAT CRIME? WE'RE HERE TO SEE MR. CUBITT ABOUT A CASE.
YOU HAD BETTER COME WITH ME.

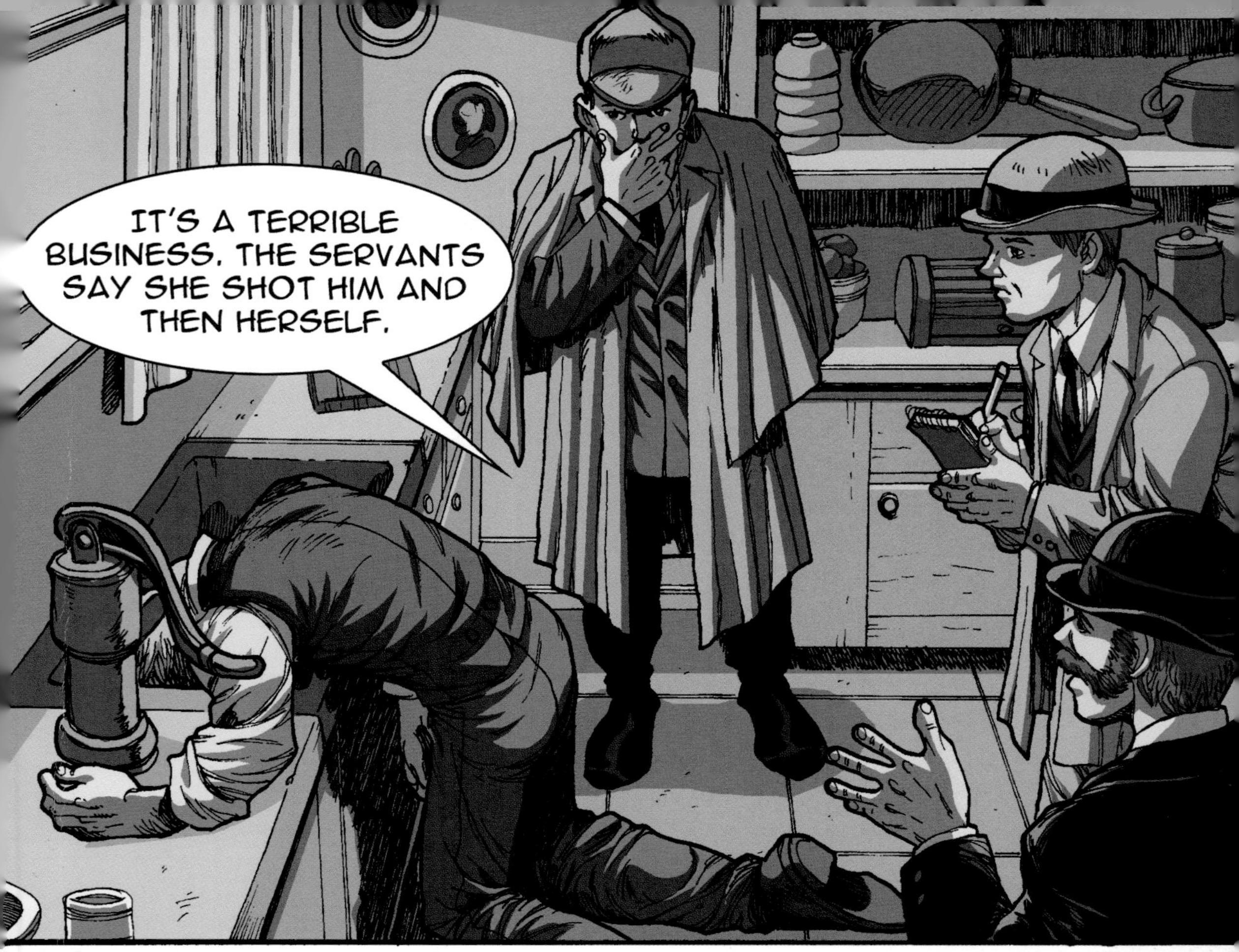
IT'S A TERRIBLE BUSINESS. THE SERVANTS SAY SHE SHOT HIM AND THEN HERSELF.

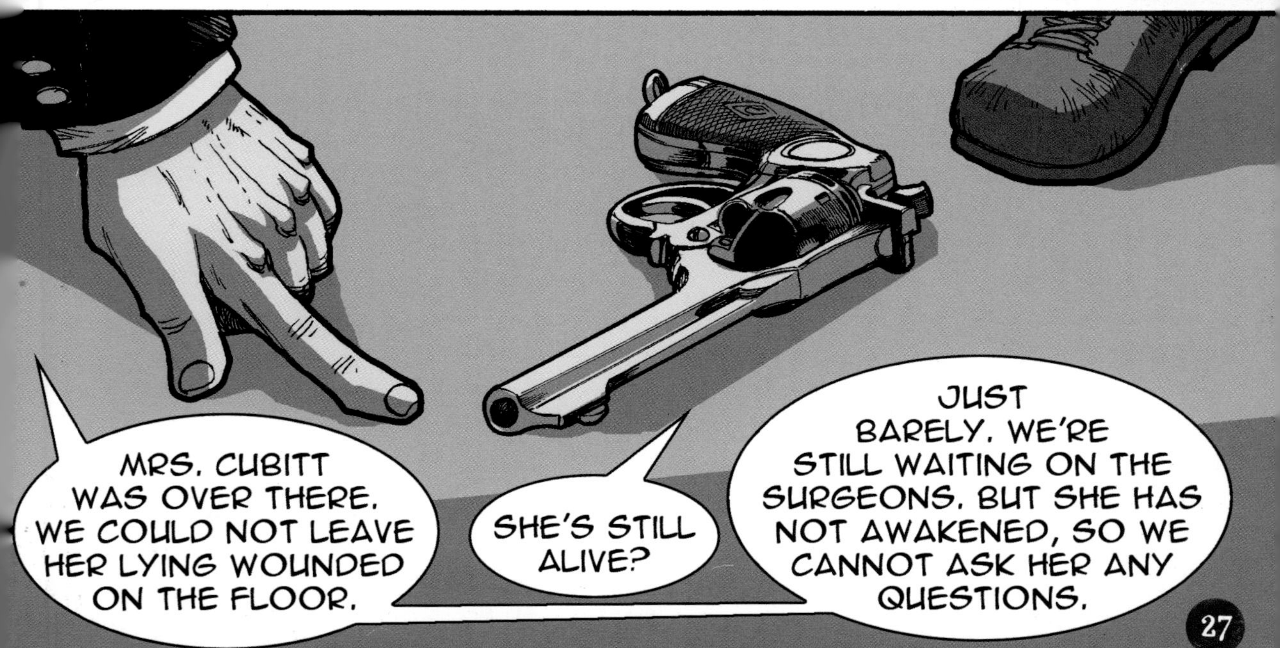
MRS. CUBITT WAS OVER THERE. WE COULD NOT LEAVE HER LYING WOUNDED ON THE FLOOR.
SHE'S STILL ALIVE?
JUST BARELY. WE'RE STILL WAITING ON THE SURGEONS. BUT SHE HAS NOT AWAKENED, SO WE CANNOT ASK HER ANY QUESTIONS.

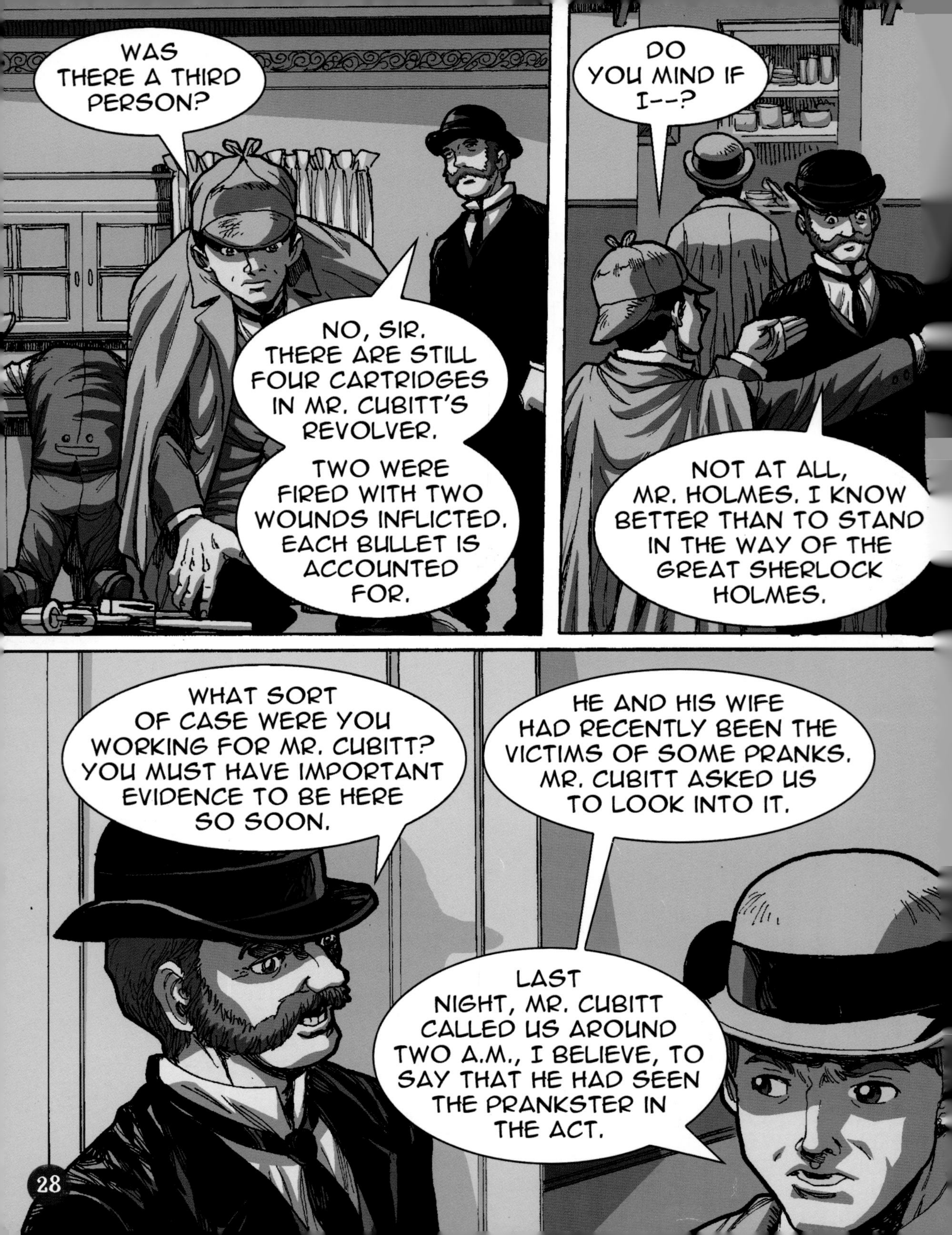
WAS THERE A THIRD PERSON?
NO, SIR. THERE ARE STILL FOUR CARTRIDGES IN MR. CUBITT'S REVOLVER.
TWO WERE FIRED WITH TWO WOUNDS INFLICTED. EACH BULLET IS ACCOUNTED FOR.
DO YOU MIND IF I--?
NOT AT ALL, MR. HOLMES. I KNOW BETTER THAN TO STAND IN THE WAY OF THE GREAT SHERLOCK HOLMES.
WHAT SORT OF CASE WERE YOU WORKING FOR MR. CUBITT? YOU MUST HAVE IMPORTANT EVIDENCE TO BE HERE SO SOON.
HE AND HIS WIFE HAD RECENTLY BEEN THE VICTIMS OF SOME PRANKS. MR. CUBITT ASKED US TO LOOK INTO IT.
LAST NIGHT, MR. CUBITT CALLED US AROUND TWO A.M., I BELIEVE, TO SAY THAT HE HAD SEEN THE PRANKSTER IN THE ACT.

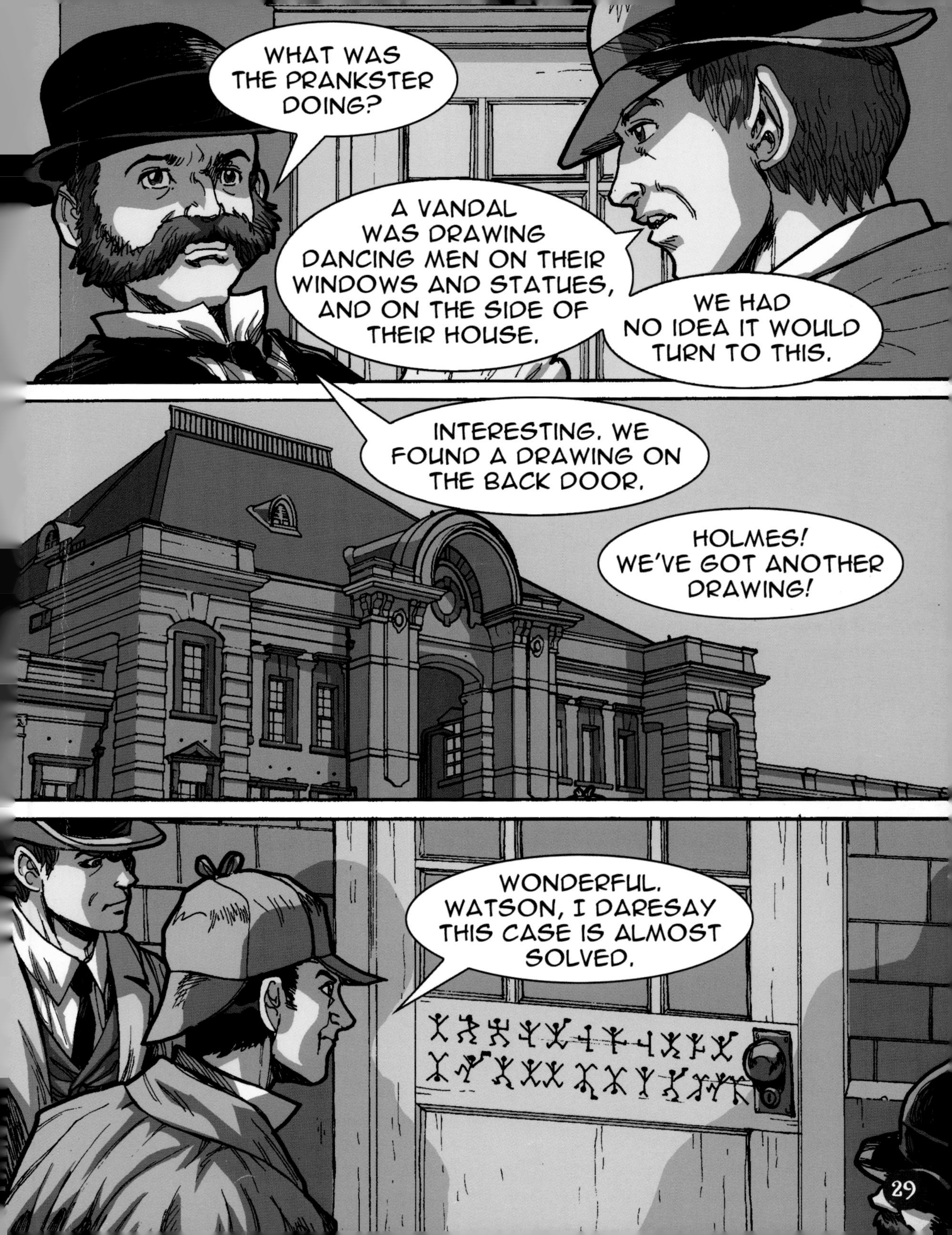
WHAT WAS THE PRANKSTER DOING?
A VANDAL WAS DRAWING DANCING MEN ON THEIR WINDOWS AND STATUES, AND ON THE SIDE OF THEIR HOUSE.
WE HAD NO IDEA IT WOULD TURN TO THIS.
INTERESTING. WE FOUND A DRAWING ON THE BACK DOOR.
HOLMES! WE'VE GOT ANOTHER DRAWING!
WONDERFUL. WATSON, I DARESAY THIS CASE IS ALMOST SOLVED.

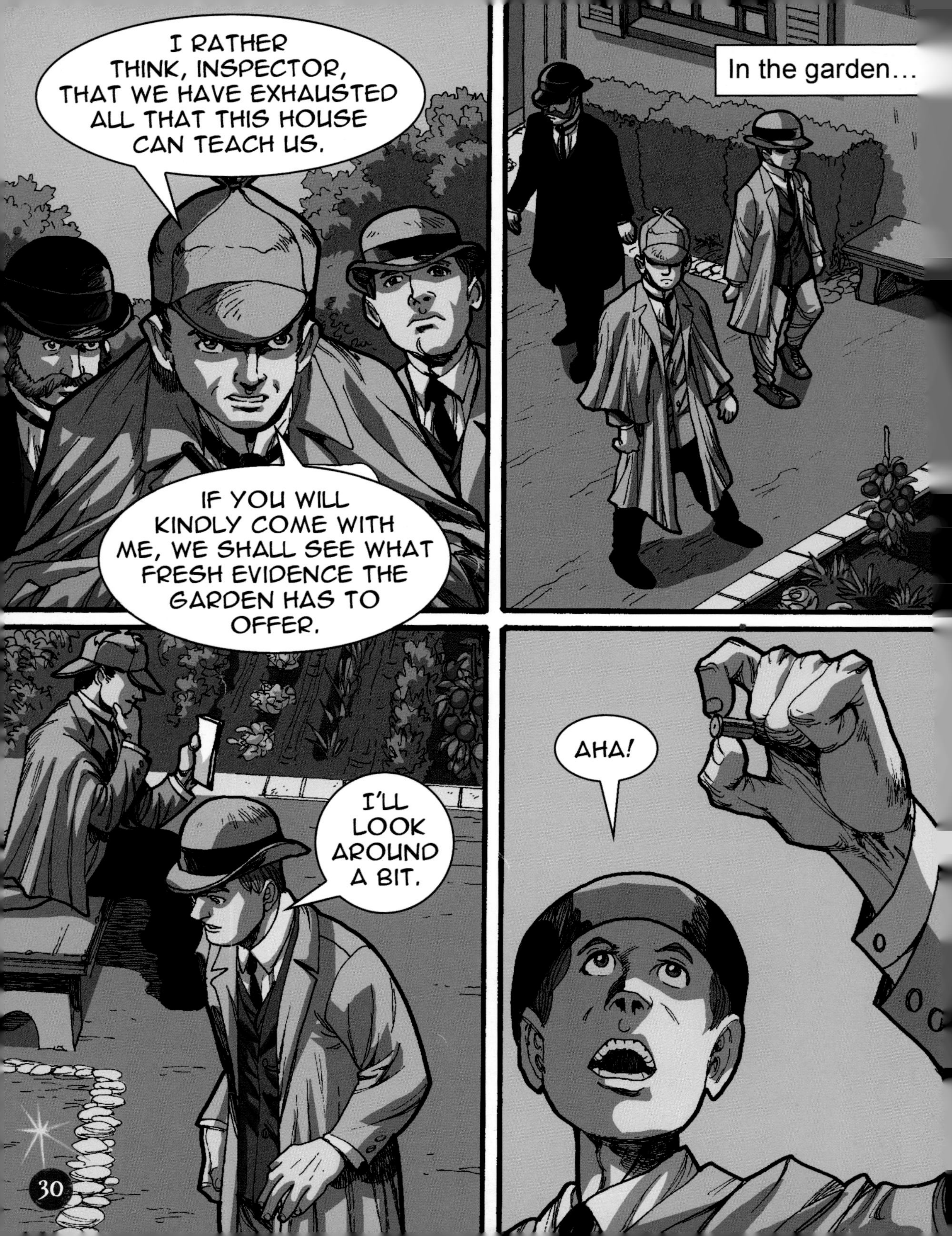
I RATHER THINK, INSPECTOR, THAT WE HAVE EXHAUSTED ALL THAT THIS HOUSE CAN TEACH US.
IF YOU WILL KINDLY COME WITH ME, WE SHALL SEE WHAT FRESH EVIDENCE THE GARDEN HAS TO OFFER.
In the garden…
I'LL LOOK AROUND A BIT.
AHA!

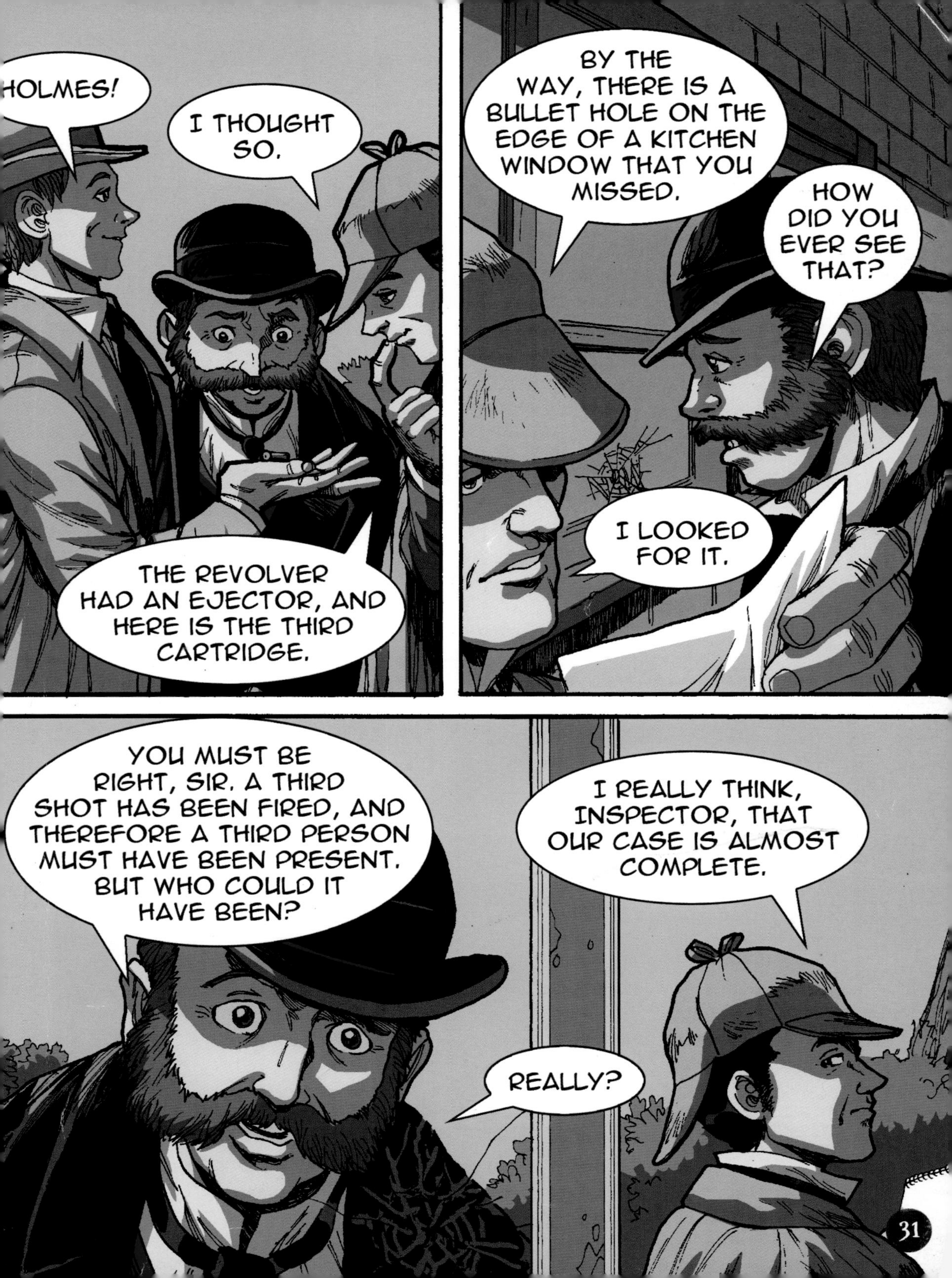
HOLMES!
I THOUGHT SO.
THE REVOLVER HAD AN EJECTOR, AND HERE IS THE THIRD CARTRIDGE.
BY THE WAY, THERE IS A BULLET HOLE ON THE EDGE OF A KITCHEN WINDOW THAT YOU MISSED.
HOW DID YOU EVER SEE THAT?
I LOOKED FOR IT.
YOU MUST BE RIGHT, SIR. A THIRD SHOT HAS BEEN FIRED, AND THEREFORE A THIRD PERSON MUST HAVE BEEN PRESENT. BUT WHO COULD IT HAVE BEEN?
I REALLY THINK, INSPECTOR, THAT OUR CASE IS ALMOST COMPLETE.
REALLY?

IS THERE AN INN IN THIS NEIGHBORHOOD KNOWN AS ELRIGE'S?

YES, ABOUT A MILE WEST.

CAPITAL! COULD YOU GET ONE OF YOUR OFFICERS TO TAKE THIS MESSAGE TO ELRIGE'S AND DELIVER IT TO A MR. ABE SLANEY?

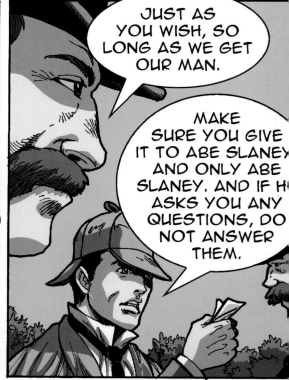

JUST AS YOU WISH, SO LONG AS WE GET OUR MAN.

MAKE SURE YOU GIVE IT TO ABE SLANEY AND ONLY ABE SLANEY. AND IF H ASKS YOU ANY QUESTIONS, DO NOT ANSWER THEM.

IF HE ASKS ABOUT MRS. CUBITT, SAY SHE IS RECOVERING WELL.

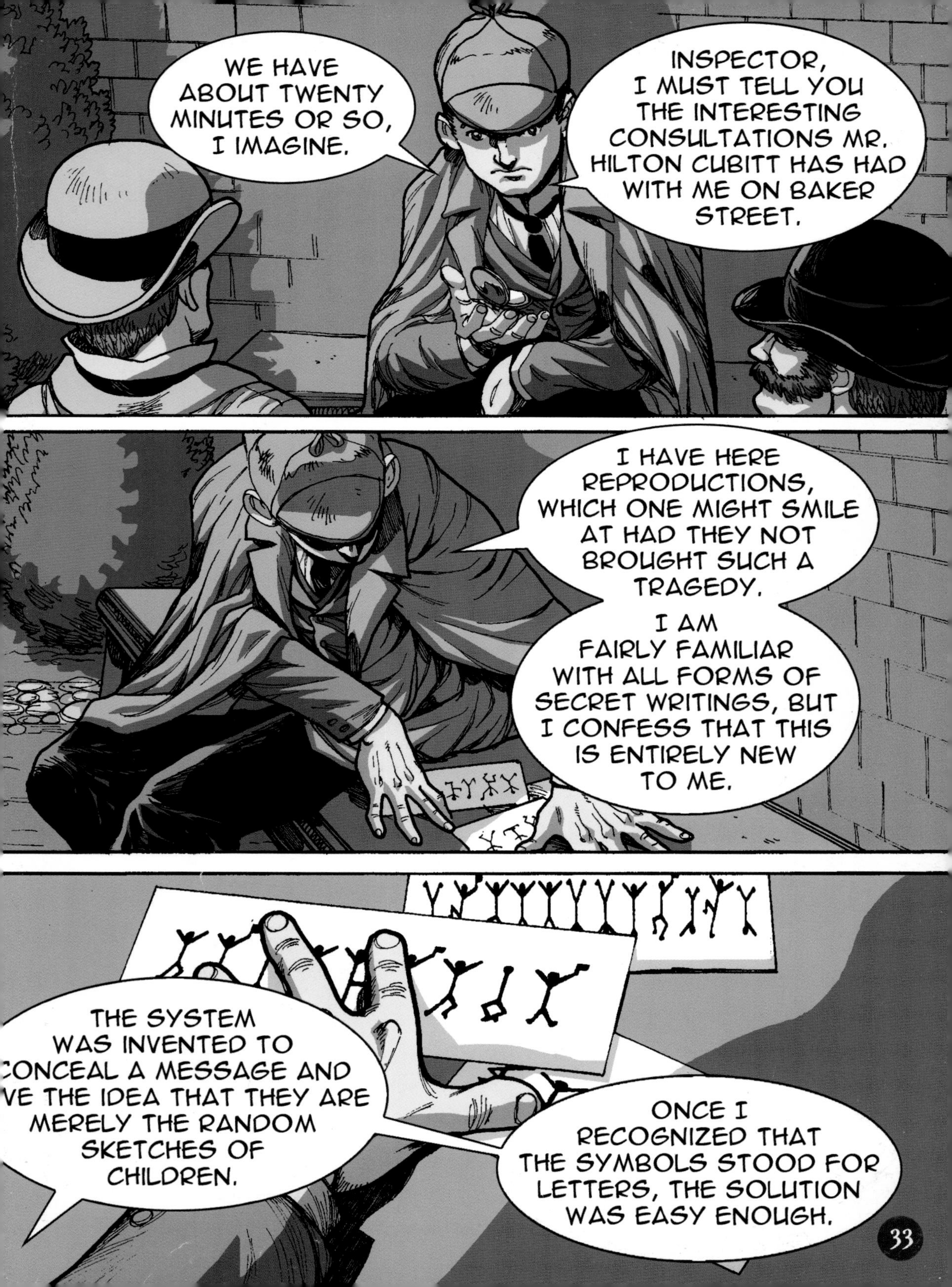
WE HAVE ABOUT TWENTY MINUTES OR SO, I IMAGINE.
INSPECTOR, I MUST TELL YOU THE INTERESTING CONSULTATIONS MR. HILTON CUBITT HAS HAD WITH ME ON BAKER STREET.
I HAVE HERE REPRODUCTIONS, WHICH ONE MIGHT SMILE AT HAD THEY NOT BROUGHT SUCH A TRAGEDY.
I AM FAIRLY FAMILIAR WITH ALL FORMS OF SECRET WRITINGS, BUT I CONFESS THAT THIS IS ENTIRELY NEW TO ME.
THE SYSTEM WAS INVENTED TO ONCEAL A MESSAGE AND VE THE IDEA THAT THEY ARE MERELY THE RANDOM SKETCHES OF CHILDREN.
ONCE I RECOGNIZED THAT THE SYMBOLS STOOD FOR LETTERS, THE SOLUTION WAS EASY ENOUGH.

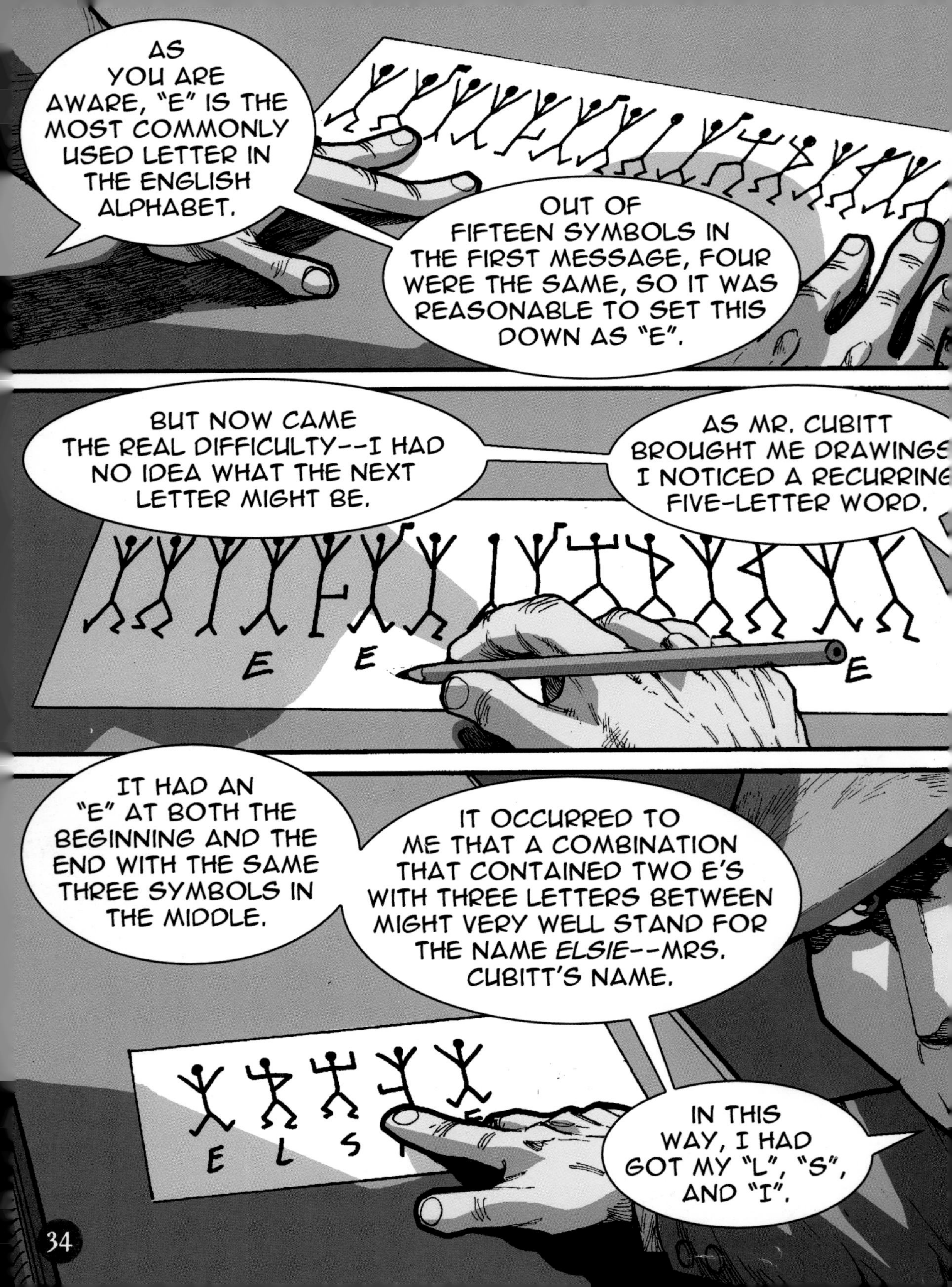
AS YOU ARE AWARE, "E" IS THE MOST COMMONLY USED LETTER IN THE ENGLISH ALPHABET.
OUT OF FIFTEEN SYMBOLS IN THE FIRST MESSAGE, FOUR WERE THE SAME, SO IT WAS REASONABLE TO SET THIS DOWN AS "E".
BUT NOW CAME THE REAL DIFFICULTY--I HAD NO IDEA WHAT THE NEXT LETTER MIGHT BE.
AS MR. CUBITT BROUGHT ME DRAWINGS I NOTICED A RECURRING FIVE-LETTER WORD.
E
E
E
IT HAD AN "E" AT BOTH THE BEGINNING AND THE END WITH THE SAME THREE SYMBOLS IN THE MIDDLE.
IT OCCURRED TO ME THAT A COMBINATION THAT CONTAINED TWO E'S WITH THREE LETTERS BETWEEN MIGHT VERY WELL STAND FOR THE NAME *ELSIE*--MRS. CUBITT'S NAME.
E L S
IN THIS WAY, I HAD GOT MY "L", "S", AND "I".

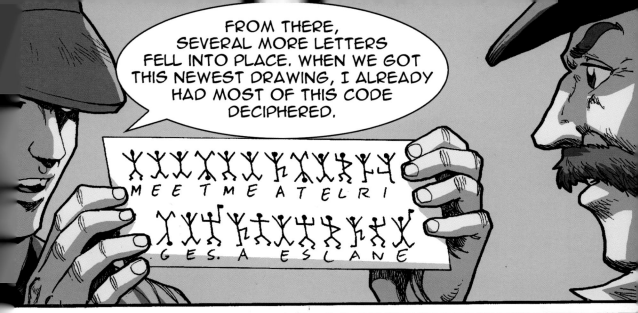

FROM THERE, SEVERAL MORE LETTERS FELL INTO PLACE. WHEN WE GOT THIS NEWEST DRAWING, I ALREADY HAD MOST OF THIS CODE DECIPHERED.

M E E T M E A T E L R I

. G E S . A E S L A N E

FOR THE NAME, I HAD A-BLANK-E. ABE IS AN AMERICAN NICKNAME, AND SINCE A LETTER FROM AMERICA HAD BEEN THE STARTING POINT OF ALL THE TROUBLE, IT SEEMED TO CONNECT.

AND SLANEY IS A COMMON AMERICAN SURNAME, TOO.

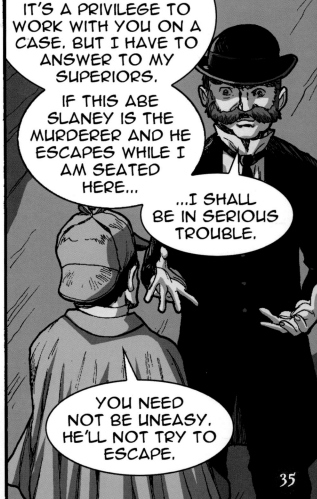

IT'S A PRIVILEGE TO WORK WITH YOU ON A CASE. BUT I HAVE TO ANSWER TO MY SUPERIORS.

IF THIS ABE SLANEY IS THE MURDERER AND HE ESCAPES WHILE I AM SEATED HERE...

...I SHALL BE IN SERIOUS TROUBLE.

YOU NEED NOT BE UNEASY. HE'LL NOT TRY TO ESCAPE.

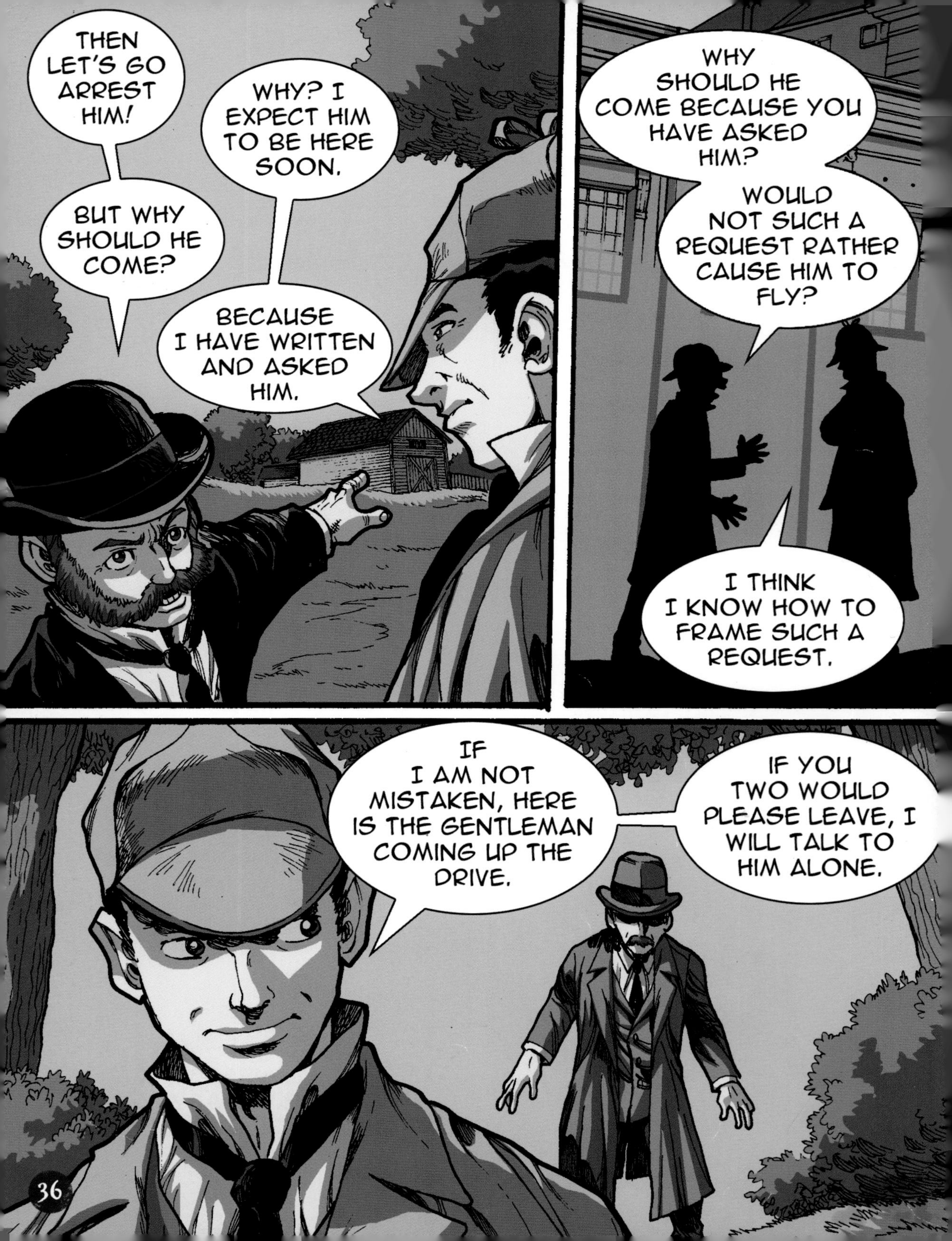
THEN LET'S GO ARREST HIM!
WHY? I EXPECT HIM TO BE HERE SOON.
BUT WHY SHOULD HE COME?
BECAUSE I HAVE WRITTEN AND ASKED HIM.
WHY SHOULD HE COME BECAUSE YOU HAVE ASKED HIM?
WOULD NOT SUCH A REQUEST RATHER CAUSE HIM TO FLY?
I THINK I KNOW HOW TO FRAME SUCH A REQUEST.
IF I AM NOT MISTAKEN, HERE IS THE GENTLEMAN COMING UP THE DRIVE.
IF YOU TWO WOULD PLEASE LEAVE, I WILL TALK TO HIM ALONE.

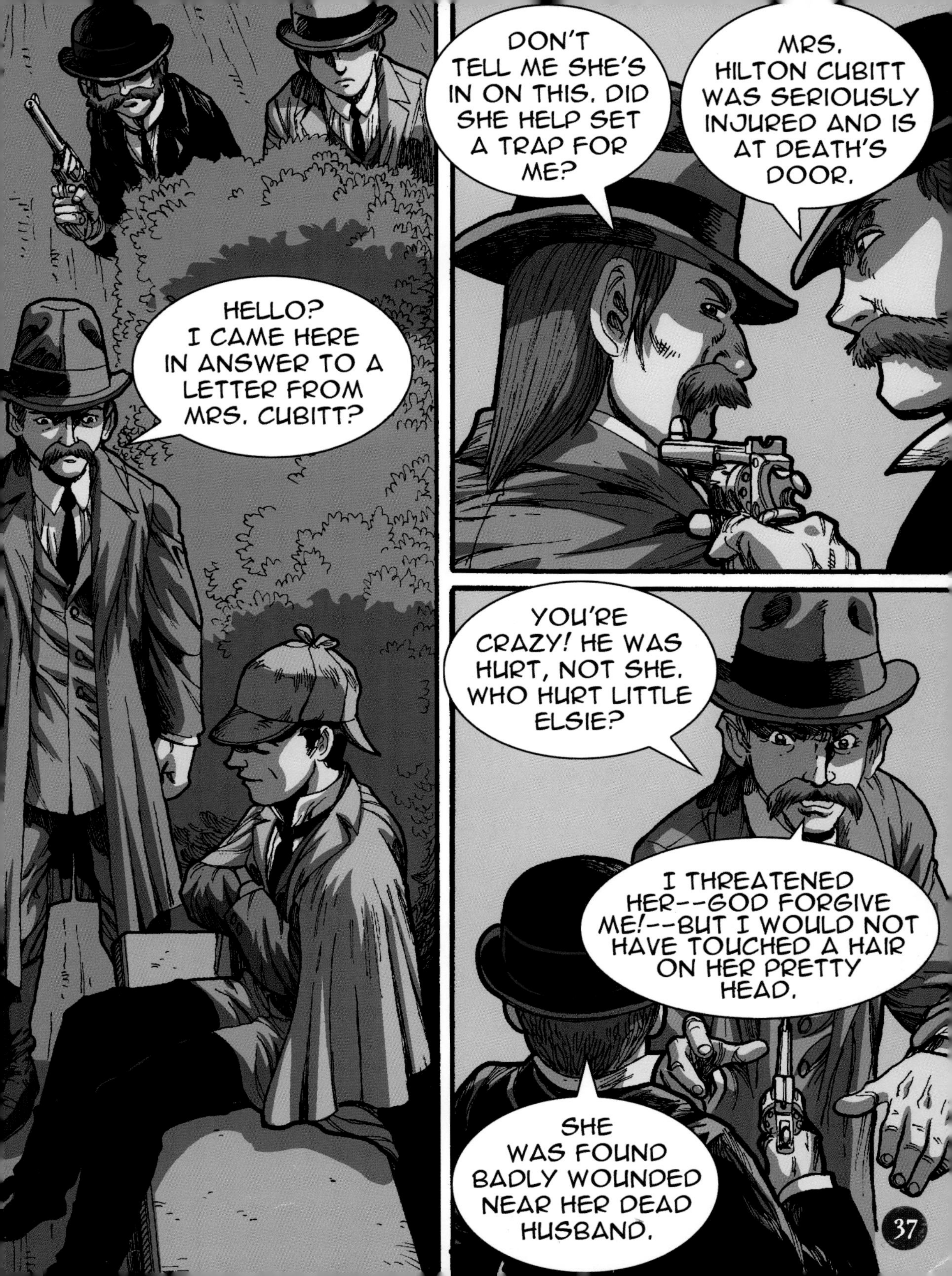
HELLO? I CAME HERE IN ANSWER TO A LETTER FROM MRS. CUBITT?
DON'T TELL ME SHE'S IN ON THIS. DID SHE HELP SET A TRAP FOR ME?
MRS. HILTON CUBITT WAS SERIOUSLY INJURED AND IS AT DEATH'S DOOR.
YOU'RE CRAZY! HE WAS HURT, NOT SHE. WHO HURT LITTLE ELSIE?
SHE WAS FOUND BADLY WOUNDED NEAR HER DEAD HUSBAND.
I THREATENED HER--GOD FORGIVE ME!--BUT I WOULD NOT HAVE TOUCHED A HAIR ON HER PRETTY HEAD.

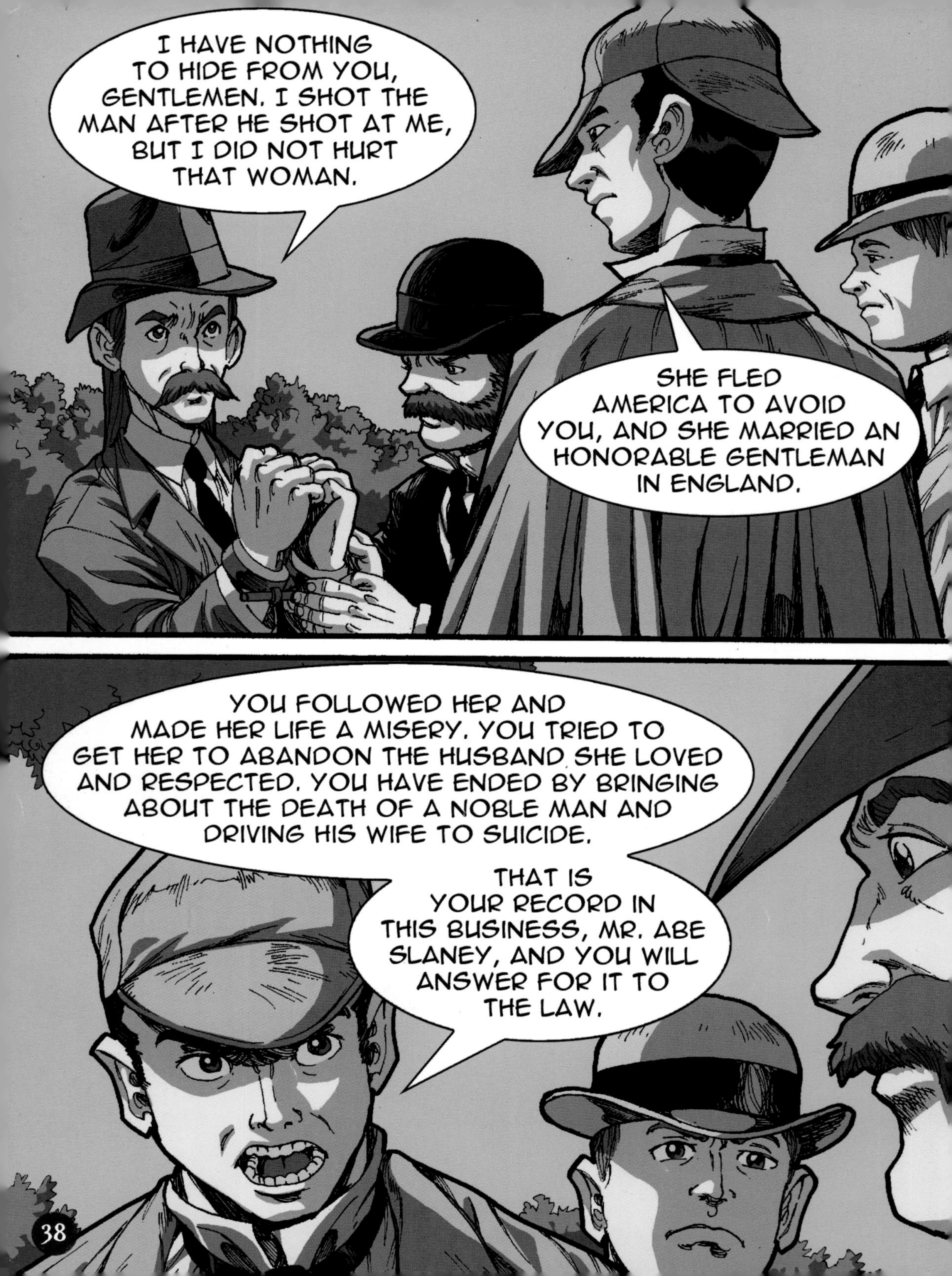
I HAVE NOTHING TO HIDE FROM YOU, GENTLEMEN. I SHOT THE MAN AFTER HE SHOT AT ME, BUT I DID NOT HURT THAT WOMAN.
SHE FLED AMERICA TO AVOID YOU, AND SHE MARRIED AN HONORABLE GENTLEMAN IN ENGLAND.
YOU FOLLOWED HER AND MADE HER LIFE A MISERY. YOU TRIED TO GET HER TO ABANDON THE HUSBAND SHE LOVED AND RESPECTED. YOU HAVE ENDED BY BRINGING ABOUT THE DEATH OF A NOBLE MAN AND DRIVING HIS WIFE TO SUICIDE.
THAT IS YOUR RECORD IN THIS BUSINESS, MR. ABE SLANEY, AND YOU WILL ANSWER FOR IT TO THE LAW.

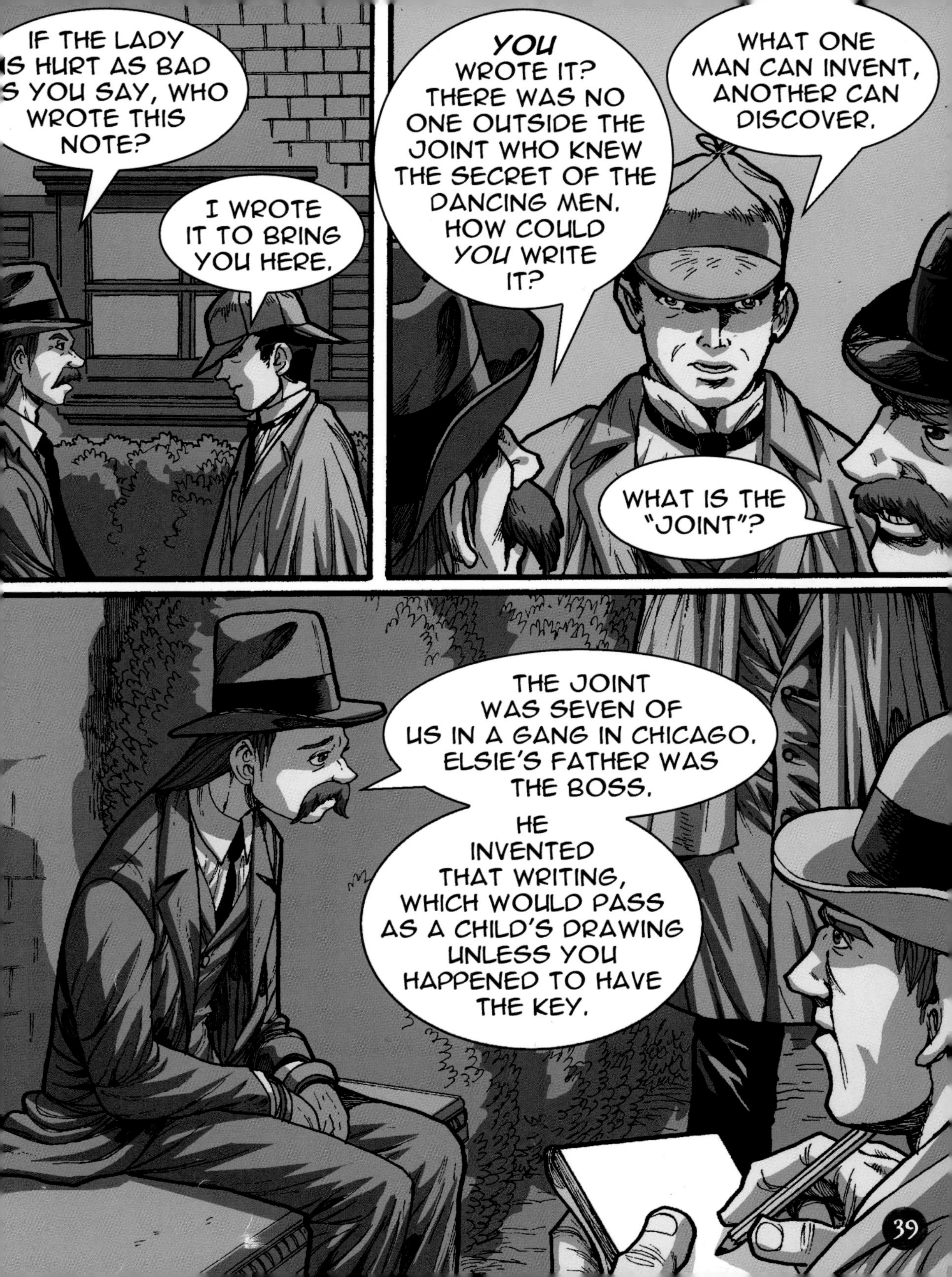
IF THE LADY IS HURT AS BAD AS YOU SAY, WHO WROTE THIS NOTE?
I WROTE IT TO BRING YOU HERE.
YOU WROTE IT? THERE WAS NO ONE OUTSIDE THE JOINT WHO KNEW THE SECRET OF THE DANCING MEN. HOW COULD *YOU* WRITE IT?
WHAT ONE MAN CAN INVENT, ANOTHER CAN DISCOVER.
WHAT IS THE "JOINT"?
THE JOINT WAS SEVEN OF US IN A GANG IN CHICAGO. ELSIE'S FATHER WAS THE BOSS.
HE INVENTED THAT WRITING, WHICH WOULD PASS AS A CHILD'S DRAWING UNLESS YOU HAPPENED TO HAVE THE KEY.

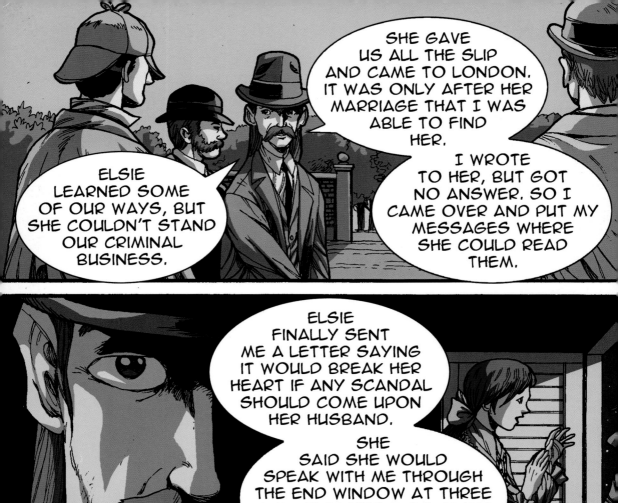

SHE GAVE US ALL THE SLIP AND CAME TO LONDON. IT WAS ONLY AFTER HER MARRIAGE THAT I WAS ABLE TO FIND HER.

I WROTE TO HER, BUT GOT NO ANSWER. SO I CAME OVER AND PUT MY MESSAGES WHERE SHE COULD READ THEM.

ELSIE LEARNED SOME OF OUR WAYS, BUT SHE COULDN'T STAND OUR CRIMINAL BUSINESS.

ELSIE FINALLY SENT ME A LETTER SAYING IT WOULD BREAK HER HEART IF ANY SCANDAL SHOULD COME UPON HER HUSBAND.

SHE SAID SHE WOULD SPEAK WITH ME THROUGH THE END WINDOW AT THREE A.M., IF I WOULD GO AWAY AFTERWARD AND LEAVE HER IN PEACE.

SHE TRIED TO BRIBE ME TO LEAVE ENGLAND.

THIS MADE ME MAD, AND I TRIED TO PULL HER THROUGH THE WINDOW.

AT THAT MOMENT, THE HUSBAND RUSHED IN WITH HIS REVOLVER.

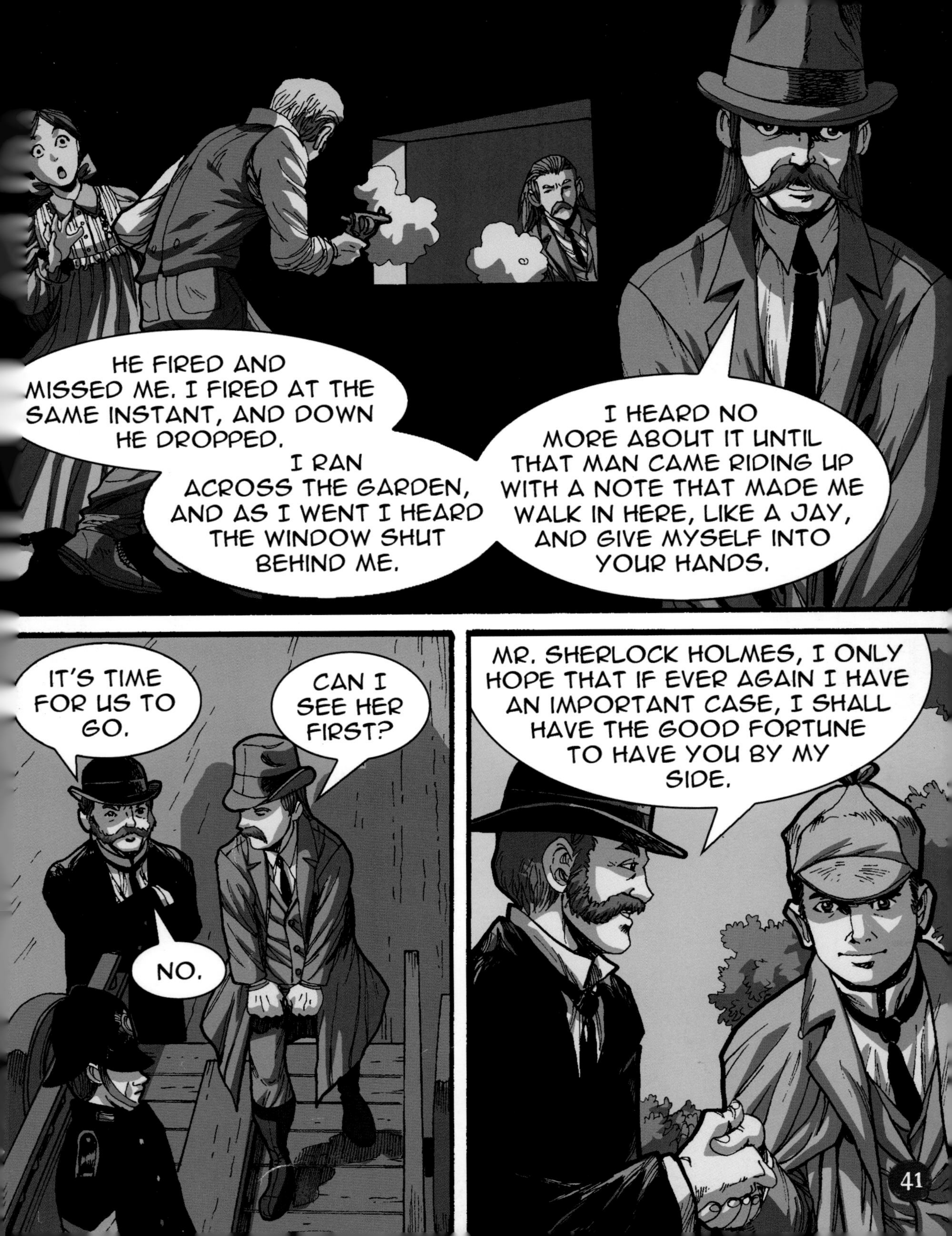
HE FIRED AND MISSED ME. I FIRED AT THE SAME INSTANT, AND DOWN HE DROPPED.
I RAN ACROSS THE GARDEN, AND AS I WENT I HEARD THE WINDOW SHUT BEHIND ME.
I HEARD NO MORE ABOUT IT UNTIL THAT MAN CAME RIDING UP WITH A NOTE THAT MADE ME WALK IN HERE, LIKE A JAY, AND GIVE MYSELF INTO YOUR HANDS.
IT'S TIME FOR US TO GO.
CAN I SEE HER FIRST?
NO.
MR. SHERLOCK HOLMES, I ONLY HOPE THAT IF EVER AGAIN I HAVE AN IMPORTANT CASE, I SHALL HAVE THE GOOD FORTUNE TO HAVE YOU BY MY SIDE.

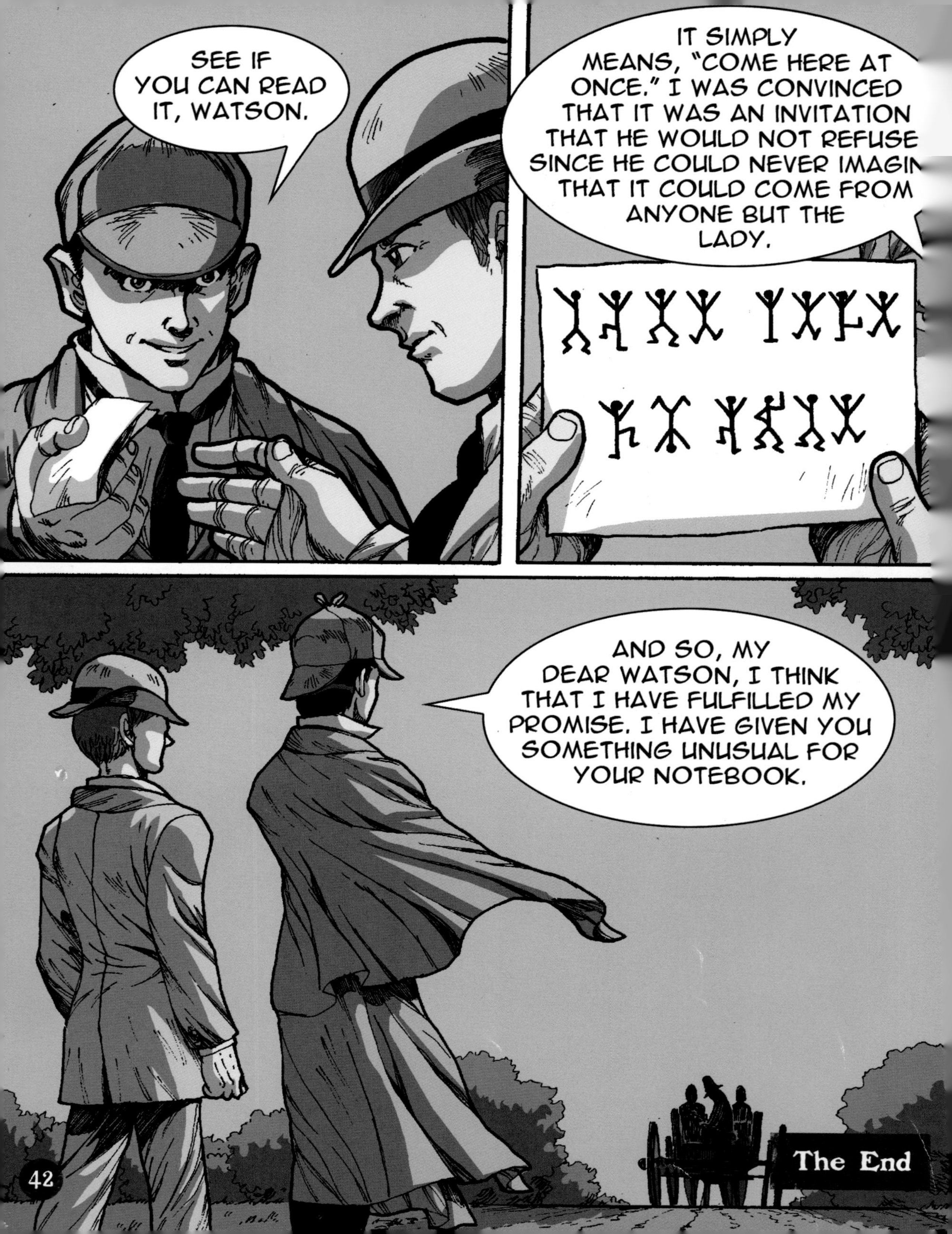
SEE IF YOU CAN READ IT, WATSON.
IT SIMPLY MEANS, "COME HERE AT ONCE." I WAS CONVINCED THAT IT WAS AN INVITATION THAT HE WOULD NOT REFUSE SINCE HE COULD NEVER IMAGIN THAT IT COULD COME FROM ANYONE BUT THE LADY.
AND SO, MY DEAR WATSON, I THINK THAT I HAVE FULFILLED MY PROMISE. I HAVE GIVEN YOU SOMETHING UNUSUAL FOR YOUR NOTEBOOK.
The End

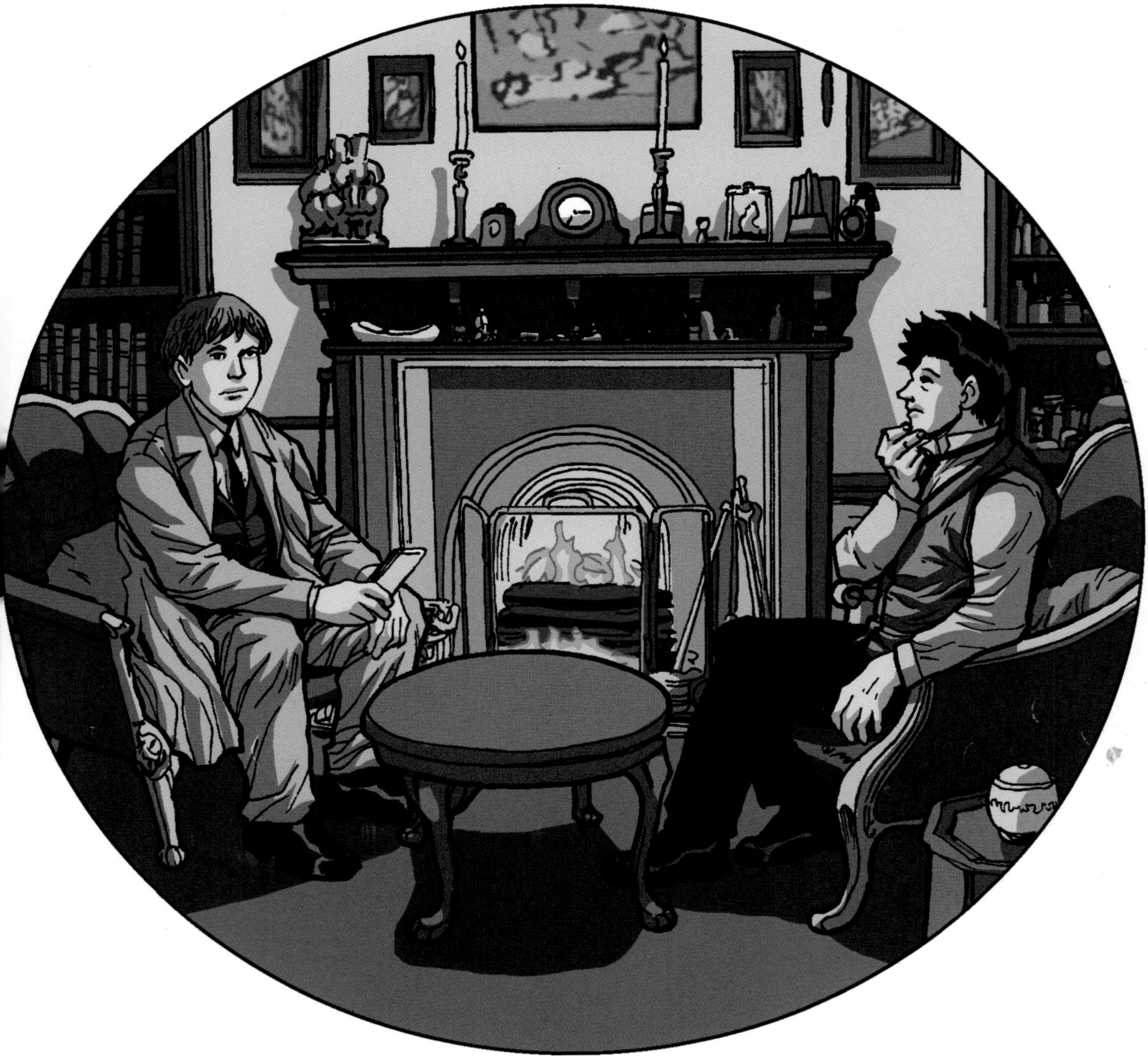

How to Draw
Sherlock Holmes

by Ben Dunn

Step 1: Use a pencil to draw a simple framework. You can start with a stick figure! Then add circles, ovals, and cylinders to get the basic form. Getting the simple shapes in place is the beginning to solving any great case.

Step 2: Time to add to Sherlock's look. Use the shapes you started with to fill in his clothes. Use guidelines to add circles for the eyes. And don't forget the hair.

Step 3: Now you can go in with a pen and start inking Sherlock. Fill in all the details and fix any mistakes. Let the ink dry to avoid smudges, then erase any pencil marks. Sherlock is ready for some color, so grab your markers and get started!

Glossary

absurd - to be impossibly unreasonable or unsound.

confidence - a relationship of trust.

consultation - the act of meeting to discuss an issue.

dazed - stunned.

decipher - to interpret or translate by using a key.

disclosure - something, such as information, that is made known to the public.

ergo - a term meaning therefore.

exhaust - to try out all possibilities.

hieroglyph - a character in a system of writing using mainly pictures.

nickname - a descriptive name given to a person by friends, family, or the media.

scandal - an action that shocks people and disgraces those connected with it.

surname - the name used by all members of a family. In America, the surname is a person's last name.

systematic - using an orderly procedure or plan to review something.

Web Sites

To learn more about Sir Arthur Conan Doyle, visit ABDO Group online at **www.abdopublishing.com**. Web sites about Doyle are featured on our Book Links page. These links are routinely monitored and updated to provide the most current information available.

About the Author

Arthur Conan Doyle was born on May 22, 1859, in Edinburgh, Scotland. He was the second of Charles Altamont and Mary Foley Doyle's ten children. In 1868, Conan Doyle began his schooling in England. Eight years later, he returned to Scotland.

Upon his return, Doyle entered the University of Edinburgh's medical school, where he became a doctor in 1885. That year, he married Louisa Hawkins. Together they had two children.

While a medical student, Doyle was impressed when his professor observed the tiniest details of a patient's condition. Doyle later wrote stories where his most famous character, Sherlock Holmes, used this same technique to solve mysteries. Holmes first appeared in *A Study in Scarlet* in 1887 and was immediately popular.

Between 1887 and 1927, Doyle wrote 66 stories and 3 novels about Holmes. He also wrote other fiction and nonfiction novels throughout his life. In 1902, Doyle was knighted for his work in a field hospital in the South African War. Four years later, Louisa died. Doyle married Jean Leckie in 1907, and they had three children together.

Sir Arthur Conan Doyle died on July 7, 1930, in Sussex, England. Today, Doyle's famous character, Sherlock Holmes, is honored with societies around the world that pay tribute to the detective.

Additional Works

A Study in Scarlet (1887)

The Mystery of Cloomber (1889)

The Firm of Girdlestone (1890)

The White Company (1891)

The Adventures of Sherlock Holmes (1891-92)

The Memoirs of Sherlock Holmes (1892-93)

Round the Red Lamp (1894)

The Stark Munro Letters (1895)

The Great Boer War (1900)

The Hound of the Baskervilles (1901-02)

The Return of Sherlock Holmes (1903-04)

Through the Magic Door (1907)

The Crime of the Congo (1909)

The Coming of the Fairies (1922)

Memories and Adventures (1924)

The Case-Book of Sherlock Holmes (1921-1927)

About the Adapters

Author

Vincent Goodwin earned his B.A. in Drama and Communications from Trinity University in San Antonio. He is the writer of three plays as well as the cowriter of the comic book *Pirates vs. Ninjas II*. Goodwin is also an accomplished journalist, having won several awards for his work as a columnist and reporter.

Illustrator

Ben Dunn founded Antarctic Press, one of the largest comic companies in the United States. His works appear in Marvel and Image comics. He is best known for his series *Ninja High School* and *Warrior Nun Areala*.